D1571344

turtle
creek

Return of
The Long Riders

Return of
The Long Riders

CLIFF FARRELL

Sagebrush
Large Print Westerns

Library of Congress Cataloging in Publication Data

Farrell, Cliff.
    Return of the long riders / Cliff Farrell.
p. cm.
ISBN 1-57490-235-0 (hardcover : alk. Paper)
    1. Large Type Books I. Tiyle
PS3556.A766 R48 1999
813'.54 21—dc21

                                  99-044940

Cataloguing in Publication Data is available from
the British Library and the National Library of Australia.

Sagebrush Large Print Westerns are published in the United States and Canada by Thomas T. Beeler, Publisher, Box 659, Hampton Falls, New Hampshire 03844-0659. ISBN 1-57490-235-0

Published in the United Kingdom, Eire, and the Republic of South Africa by Isis Publishing Ltd, 7 Centremead, Osney Mead, Oxford OX2 0ES England. ISBN 0-7531-6131 X

Published in Australia and New Zealand by Australian Large Print Audio & Video Pty Ltd, 17 Mohr Street, Tullamarine, Victoria, 3043, Australia. ISBN 1-86442-356-0

Manufactured in the United States of America by Sheridan Books in Chelsea, Michigan.

Return of
The Long Riders

CHAPTER 1

DEL KITTRIDGE HAD LOST TRACK OF TIME. HE DIDN'T realize he was returning home on a holiday until he rode near enough to Combabi to see the bunting and the flags and hear the firecrackers and the pistols that were being touched off in town.

It was Independence Day. When he had been a ranch boy, growing up in the Combabi, the Fourth of July and Christmas had been the days to look forward to for him. That didn't seem so long in the past. Yet today in this year of 1904 it was as though it had been in another life.

The memories of boyhood were the best memories, but time had turned them bittersweet. All he knew now was that he was coming home and that this was not the season of good will toward mankind. Not with the. summer sun broiling down on him from the noon sky, and the rugged flats and mountains of the border reflecting the glare.

Combabi showed little change during the half dozen years he had been away. Its fringes had advanced slightly farther into the flats, and the roofs of a few new buildings lifted in the heart of the` town. The new structures were frame-built instead of the adobe of the past. Some were even of brick as though the builders were sure they were there to stay.

He could have told them they might be mistaken. He knew what this country could do to the ambitions of men. He had seen the grudges and the feuds.

But when he rode into Jefferson Street the years rolled back and he felt that he was really home. They were beginning to line up for the parade, and that was as

1

it should be, for the procession always marched down Jefferson Street at noon on the Fourth. Most everyone who felt like parading took part in it.

The dozen members of Otto Schneider's Silver Comet Band were gathered around a beer keg in the coolness of Rezin Bartee's blacksmith shop, fortifying themselves before donning their black velvet shakos and red jackets to lead the procession.

In sidestreets, cowpunchers clad in their gaudiest, with saddle gear aglitter, were waiting to ride to the music of brass bands. Ranch rigs, festooned with bunting and streamers, were waiting too, the ladies clad in white gowns. Some of their menfolk wore frock coats and silk hats.

There were many Army uniforms along the busy sidewalks and Del saw a mounted U. S. Cavalry band drawn up in Bricker's lumberyard, prepared to add martial music to the festivities. The soldiers were from Fort Griffin, a hundred miles east. The merchants of Combabi were enjoying a business boom from military payrolls since the Army had moved in to see that Juan Torreón and other *bandidos* did not come raiding across the border with their wild *insurrectos*.

He rode to Tim Buttons' livery, which, for the first time in his memory, was painted and looked prosperous.

"I didn't expect a welcome like this," he said to the owner as he dismounted in he dimness of the wagon tunnel.

He dragged his hat from his head. It was a Mexican sombrero, with a peak shaped like a chocolate drop. It was old and limp with weather and wear and had two holes in the brim that looked like bullet holes—which indeed they were. Those marks had been placed there in the name of independence also, but they had not been

2

fired in a spirit of revelry. These were the teeth-marks of combat.

He tenderly kneaded at the bloodless streak the sweatband had left on his forehead. "A nice welcome," he added. "And I appreciate it. I appreciate it right down to the depths of my gizzard."

Tim Buttons, a dour, parchment-skinned man, reached for the bridle to lead Del's horse away. He hadn't as yet recognized his visitor in the shadow of the barn. "You almost missed your own parade, friend," he said. "You're a little late getting—"

He went silent, staring.

"You seem upset, Tim," Del said.

Tim Buttons fought his Adam's Am's apple for a moment then got a grip on himself. "My place is full up," be said. "I can't take in another horse."

"I see that you remember me," Del said.

"Yeah," said Buttons. "There're a lot of others that will too."

"It's always nice to be remembered by old acquaintances," Del said.

He looked around. Every stall was occupied. The feed corral at the rear was crowded with animals. The saddle racks in the stable were filled with rigging.

Del drew his saddle from his horse and swung it atop another on the racks. It had been a fine hull of the light, though make used only by officers in a crack outfit in the Mexican Rurales. Del had salvaged it from the dead, horse of its dead owner on a battlefield at a place called El Camay. Both its saber scabbard and pistol holster were empty. Del had come out of Mexico unarmed.

He opened the door of the nearest stall, which contained a handsome Morgan gelding, and hazed the animal toward the open corral. The Morgan objected,

3

letting fly with both hoofs, but Del had anticipated that and was well in the clear. He slapped the animal with his sombrero and sent it to join the others in the hot sun.

Its brand consisted of two stars, small and neat, burned on the left hip. "Well, well!" he said. "A Camden *caballo*! Even their damned horses are raised to believe they're better than the common run."

Tim Buttons had watched in lowering silence, but had made no move to interfere. "That's Quinn's mount," he said gloomily. "Quinn won't like havin' his hawss turned out."

Del gave him a slanting look and he quit talking. Del led his mount into the vacated stall and removed the bridle. The horse, a tough steeldust with a considerable strain of mustang, was lean and jaded from long, hard miles. Sweat and dust caked its legs and flanks.

Del brought water in a pail from the trough and the steeldust drink, rationing it at intervals until the horse had cooled and could fill up safely. He found a sponge., and soaked the dust and dried mud from fetlocks and quarters. The steeldust began to revive and nuzzle the sponge, snorting with pleasure. Del rubbed it down with a clean feed sack and forked in hay.

"I'll be back," he told Tim Buttons. "Maybe in an, hour. Maybe not 'til tomorrow. But I'll be back."

"If I was you" Buttons said, "I'd keep ridin'. You'll do yourself no good, comin' back to the Combabi."

"See to it that my horse is still in the stall and has been kept fed and watered," Del said. "He deserves the best."

He walked out of the livery into the glare of the sun. He sighed a little, feeling his weariness, feeling the cruel weight of the heat. He needed a shave and a bath. His feet were swollen in his boots. Dust was thick inside

4

his shirt.

He walked toward Sun House, the hotel that was the pride of Combabi. It rose three stories, and was topped by a clock tower. Its steam-driven elevator had been the marvel of its day and cowboys had come from far-distant ranges to take a chance on riding in the contraption.

Like most of the better business establishments in Combabi, it had been built by Walsh Camden. He had named it Sun House as complementary to his Two Star ranch. The names of lesser satellites were numerous on the signs of business places in the narrow principal street: the Planet Cafe, the Meteor Saddle Shop, the Aurora Mercantile.

A glistening black barouche, decked with bunting and a blanket of flowers, stood at the passenger step in front of Sun House. A coachman in livery waited on the driver's seat in charge of spirited hackneys whose harness bore colored pompons.

Alongside the barouche, two spectacular palominos, with combed and kinked manes, waited, bearing show-piece saddles and headstalls of tooled leather, embossed with hammered silver.

The sidewalk was crowded with bystanders who had gathered to admire the saddles and the palominos. Del could remember back into his boyhood when he had stood there also, dazzled and wishing for nothing more in the world than to own such magnificence. He had watched Quinn and Cullen Camden ride those saddles in the parades from the time they were big enough to be tied to the stirrup leathers.

Quinn and Cullen would ride the palominos today, of course, and the days when they had to be tied down were long in the past. Other Camdens would sit in the

5

barouche, along with whoever was mayor of Combabi at present, and some other dignitary.

It had always been that way in the Combabi. The Camdens always held the center of attention and were surrounded by lesser lights, just as this town had been the satellite of Two Star's wealth.

However, there would be one important flaw in the pattern this time. The king himself would be missing. Walsh Camden, the austere, aristocratic head of the family, would not be present to ride as usual in the stately carriage. He was, in fact, a prisoner in rags in a filthy dungeon in a small village in Mexico. Walsh Camden faced death by a firing squad and Del was the only person in the waiting crowd who knew this.

The only thing that might save Walsh Camden from the Mausers of Juan Torreón's *insurrectos* was a message Del carried in the peak of his ragged hat, wrapped in a scrap of oilskin.

He mounted the marble steps and entered the wide lobby of Sun House. The davenports and leather chairs were occupied by ladies in lawn and silk and beribboned bonnets The place was blue with the cigar smoke from men in wilting, starched collars. All of them were waiting too, waiting for the Camdens to appear from the suite they always occupied on the third floor when in town.

Sun House was accustomed to dusty, saddleworn men. Little notice was taken of him for a moment, in spite of the clash of his appearance with the general festive attire.

A man turned, staring after him. Another head turned. Then many more. A ripple of excitement surged across the lobby.

The clerk took a step or two toward the swing gate

6

that would permit him to leave the protection of his marble counter and block Del's path. He thought better of it, and stayed back of the barrier. "You there!" he stammered. "Now just a minute!"

Del looked at him. "I'll want a room and a tub, George," he said. "I'll be back directly to sign the register."

He ignored the gilded door of the elevator, preferring the more reliable curving marble stairs. He left a lake of staring faces in the lobby. And complete silence.

He appreciated the soft carpet that lined both the hall of the second floor and the next flight of stairs that carried him to the top level. He had not trod on carpet in months. Not since he had entered a town named Santa Rosalia which had been looted by Juan Torreón's *cucarachas*, or cockroaches.

He had bivouacked in the *sala* of what had been the home of a rich *político*. The carpet he had slept on had been as soft as a woman's cheek, as limpid as water. He had slept there for twenty hours, with rich velvet tapestry that had been torn from the walls as a blanket. He had slept like the dead alongside other fighting men, sprawled among their rifles, their machetes, their bandoliers of shells and their daggers.

The recollection of that carpet in the hacienda was not the only memory of the past that came back to him as he walked to the suite whose doors were of polished cedar, with silver handles. This proximity to the Camdens revived the past.

None of the four doors bore numbers. The Camdens never occupied numbered rooms. He could hear the hum of conversation. Evidently they had guests, but he was unable to determine in which room they were being entertained.

7

He selected a door at random and knocked. It opened after a small delay. An angular, red-haired belligerant-faced Irishwoman stood glazing.

"By the saints," Del said. "It's been many a long day since I've laid eyes on such raving beauty. Sure an' an angel it is."

Maggie Riley gazed, aghast. She had been the Camdens' housekeeper for many years.

"Ye divil ye!" she gasped. "An' it would only be the old one himself that would send Dave Kittridge's impudent son here on this day!"

Then she softened. There was the shine of tears in her eyes. "Ah, David! David!" she, breathed, glancing over her shoulder to make sure they were alone in the room. "Where in the name of Heaven have you been all these years? Sure an' 'twas said the last of the Kittridges was dead."

Del kissed her on the cheek. "Do you know, Maggie," he said. "You must be the only person alive who calls me David."

"An' who would have a better right" she said. " 'twas meself that was at your dear mother's side when you were born. She would have no other name for you than that of your father's. But 'twas himself that insisted on giving you your mother's family name. David Delaney Kittridge. You were David to your mother and to me. Let others call you Del."

He patted her hand. "You'll be spoiling all of that Cork County beauty by wailing and weeping," he said. "Now, let me talk to Quinn, if he's around. This can't wait. I want to see him alone."

" 'Tis the wrong place you've come to, if you want to find Quinn Camden," she sniffed. "Try the barroom downstairs. Or some dancehall where the painted ladies are gay."

"Cullen, then," Del said.

"Then look in such places, also. But he will not be with Quinn. They do not share even their vices. Only their jealousies."

"It'll have to be The Lady herself, then. This is important, Maggie. To the Camdens, at least."

Maggie dried her eyes. " 'Tis about *him*, isn't it? You've news of *him*. The Lady is the only one you must see. She cares about him. Quinn and Cullen care only about themselves."

"What is it, Maggie?" a new voice spoke.

A young woman had entered the room by way of an inner door from the remainder of the suite. Her eyes, which were very dark and very frank, became ice-cold as she gazed at Del. She straightened hostilely. She looked him over, from head to foot, with deliberate, disdainful slowness.

She was exceedingly attractive. She wore a white gown with many ruffles and was pulling on opera-length white gloves. Her hair, which was raven-dark, was crowned by a diadem of white flowers. Her skin was tanned a good golden shade, for she spent much time on horseback.

Del had known her from childhood. Kathryn Camden was no child now. She was three or four years younger than himself, and was married now, no doubt. If so, matrimony apparently had not subdued her. She had always been a spitfire. She was Walsh Camden's niece, but was looked upon almost as his daughter. Her parents had died when she had been a baby, and she had been raised by her uncle and aunt at Two Star.

She moved to the door to confront him and Maggie Riley gave way to her. "What do *you* want?" she

9

demanded.

"Not you, above all," Del said. "Don't come any closer. You might be defiled. On the other hand, I don't particularly care for that perfume you're using. You smell like a fandango parlor, Kay."

"My name," she said, "is Miss Camden to you. Use it when you address me—which I hope won't be often."

Del's brows lifted. "You're not married? Well, I can understand that. No man would be good enough."

"What is it you want here?"

"Maggie tells me the men of the family are, let's say, occupied. I better see your aunt."

"Aunt Harriet is busy."

"Not too busy for this."

She studied him. She lowered her voice. "It's about Uncle Walsh."

Del nodded. She stepped back, motioning him to enter the room. "Come in," she said.

Del shrugged and complied. "No damned Camden ever was taught to say please," he commented.

She ignored that and closed the door. She also locked it and kept the key in her hand. "Maggie, tell Aunt Harriet to come here. And don't blurt it out in front of everybody. Hurry!"

Maggie hastened away. Presently, a tall, handsome woman entered. She wore a wide-skirted fiesta dress, and had a spray of white and red flowers pinned to her shoulder. Her hair was iron gray and was crowned by a mantilla of white Spanish lace.

Harriet Camden hesitated when she saw Del. Her gaze swung to her niece, asking a quick question. "This," she said, "is a surprise indeed."

Her first act was to make sure the door leading to the adjoining rooms was closed. She also turned the key in

10

the lock. "To make sure we're not interrupted," she said. "This is no ordinary occasion, of course. No Kittridge ever did anything that was ordinary."

Her niece spoke. "They even stole cattle in the most unorthodox ways."

"A rare talent," Del said.

"Very," Kay Camden said. "And one that inspired others to follow their example."

"What is it that brought you here Mr. Kittridge?" her aunt asked.

Del had removed his hat He brought from it the oil-skin-protected paper and handed it to her. He turned to leave, saying, "I was asked to deliver that to the Camdens."

"Wait!" Kay Camden commanded haughtily.

Del had no alternative, inasmuch as the door was locked, and she had the key in her hand. "It's like I said," he remarked. "No Camden ever learned to say please. Now, you really don't want to have that pretty door busted down, do you?"

"You wouldn't dare!" Kay Camden exclaimed.

"I'm afraid he would, Kathryn," her aunt said. "Give him the key. However, if it would not be too much trouble, Mr. Kittridge, I'll ask you to please stay a minute or two longer."

"I can't believe my ears," he said. "Surely, the Camdens aren't turning humble?"

"No," Kay Camden said tersely.

Her aunt discarded the oiled wrapper, unfolded the enclosed sheet of writing paper and read the message that was penciled.

Del had to admire her self-possession. There was breeding and also a steely inner strength in her that prohibited any outward sign of emotion. Her fingers did

11

not display the slightest tremor. They were strong fingers, but finely formed with long, carefully kept nails.

Harriet Camden had been a famous beauty, and she was still far more than ordinarily attractive. She was said to be from a blueblooded Virginia family that had first shifted to Texas and then to the southwest border in the pioneering days. Lady Camden, she was called in the Combabi. Or simply as The Lady.

She carefully read the message a second time, then looked up at Del. He realized now that beneath her outer mask, she had been hard-hit by what she had read.

"Do you know what is in this letter?" she asked.

"I wrote it," Del said.

"*You* wrote it?"

"Juan Torreón dictated it," Del said. "He can't write."

"And is this really his mark as a signature?"

"Yes. It's really a cattle brand that he used to burn on calves when he was a young vaquero. A *quién sabe* brand. He uses it as his signature."

Harriet Camden handed the message to her niece. Kay Camden had none of her aunt's repression. She seized the paper, read it with excited haste, and uttered a cry of anger and fear.

Her eyes lifted accusingly to Del. "You wrote *this*? And had the insolence to come here and deliver it personally. Why, you're as bad as he is! As this Mexican cutthroat!"

"Just a minute, Kathryn!" her aunt protested. Her voice began to shake in spite of herself. "Is this really true? Is Juan Torreón holding my husband for ransom?"

"You might call it that," Del said. "At least, he's being held until somebody turns over three hundred head of horses to Torreón."

12

"How awful!" Kay Camden cried. "And you are—!"

"Did you see my husband?" her aunt interrupted her.

"Yes," Del said.

"Is he—is he being mistreated?"

"No more than any others who are held in cells by a man like Torreón."

"That means he is—!" Kay Camden began tearfully.

"Please Kathryn!" her aunt said. "But there's been no—no—?" Her voice faltered.

"No actual torture, if that's what you're thinking," Del said.

"At least until now," Harriet Camden said. "That's what you actually mean, isn't it? I know the kind of a person Torreón is. How long ago did you see my husband?"

Del estimated it on his fingers. "Two night, three days of hard riding. At a place called Arroyo Grande. Torreón is making his headquarters there with his army. He's waiting there, hoping to build up his supplies. But it's horses he needs most of all."

"What would happen if we refuse this blackmail?"

Del eyed her stonily. "You wouldn't want me to answer that, now would you? You just said you know what kind of a man Torreón is. Maybe you really don't. Look."

He rolled up his left sleeve. A number of raw blisters stood out on the inner side of his forearm. "Torreón was smoking a cigar while I wrote that note for him. Just to make sure I paid attention, he used my arm as an ashtray."

Harriet Camden blanched. Her niece suddenly sat down in a chair, looking ill.

"But the United States government will—" Kay Camden began shakily.

13

"—help a man who tried to dicker to run horses across the line for profit?" Del said ironically. "Hardly. Walsh Camden was on illegal business. Horses are embargoed by the United States, along with other munitions of war. Your uncle is strictly on his own. He's subject to prison in this country if the Army catches him."

"Righteous talk from one of Torreón's ruffians!" Kay Camden flared.

"Ex-ruffian," Del corrected her. "I turned against him. That's as dangerous as trying to run a double-cross on him, as Walsh Camden had found out."

Harriet Camden forced her chin to rise haughtily. But it was an effort of will, and did not come from the heart. "Double-cross. What do you mean, sir?"

"Your husband went to Arroyo Grande and agreed to sell three hundred head of horses to Torreón at one hundred dollars a head in gold. Then your husband went to another *insurrecto* general. *Bandido*, rather. Northern Mexico is full of these self-styled *libertadors*. They liberate only the people from what little they have, including their lives. Your husband wrangled a better offer from an *insurrecto* named Antonio Carrosco, who is Torreón's bitter rival. Ten dollars a head more."

"That's a lie!" Kay Camden burst out. But she said it uncertainly. Like her aunt, she was forced to belabor her pride in order to act out her role as a Camden.

Del eyed her without expression. He took the key from her hand and she made no attempt to retain it. He walked to the door and unlocked it.

"Torreón learned about the deal and caught Walsh Camden before he could get back across the border. Torreón would have shot him on the spot, but he still needs horses. That's the only reason Walsh Camden is still alive."

He opened the door and stepped into the hall.

"Wait—" Harriet Camden began.

Del closed the door. The memory of the faces of The Lady and her niece stayed with him as he walked away from the door.

CHAPTER 2

THREE MEN IN SILK HATS AND FROCK COATS HAD JUST stepped from the elevator. One was Ed Donally, mayor of Combabi and also president of the Combabi National Bank. The others were also old-time business men whom Del knew. He guessed that they composed a committee that would escort Lady Camden and her niece to the waiting barouche.

They recognized him. Surprised, they paused. Ed Donally frowned and started to say something. Then he thought better of it. He motioned his companions to proceed and they pushed past Del and continued on down the corridor to the door of the Camden suite. They looked back, puzzled and frowning.

Del descended to the lobby and again found himself facing a battery of staring eyes. He ignored them, but the pressure of this curiosity was having its way with him. Combabi had placed its thumb on him and was pressing down harder and harder.

He headed for the clerk's counter but was forced to shoulder his way through cigar-smoking citizens, none of whom moved to accommodate him. He left behind him mumbling, angry, ruffled men, their fronts strewn with the ashes from their smokes.

"Just like a damned Kittridge," someone grumbled.

"I'm ready for that room now," Del said to George Watkins, the clerk. "I need all the trimmings. Forty gallons of warm water, hot towels to steam down these whiskers before I shave, bay rum and some pretty-smelling bath soap."

"We've got no accommodations," the clerk said. "We're full up."

"And even if you weren't, I wouldn't be wanted here," Del said. "That's the way of it, isn't it, George?"

The clerk turned away without answering. Del walked out of the hotel. The swarm of bystanders had increased on the sidewalk, awaiting the appearance of the Camdens. Del decided to linger for a while also. He wondered if The Lady and Kay Camden would go through with it—maintain the Camden tradition.

Stiff-necked, iron pride had stood Harriet Camden, in good stead. Even so, some of the fear and desperation had come to the surface. He knew how bitterly she must have regretted any display of weakness in the presence of anyone, particularly a Kittridge.

All during the journey out of Mexico and past the border patrols, he had looked forward with grim anticipation to delivering that message to the Camdens and watching its effect on them.

That had armored him against the hardships of that long ride, during which he had slept mainly in the saddle and had gone on short rations and lost pounds in weight.

He watched the people who were waiting to fawn on the Camdens in the hope they would be noticed. He wondered what their attitude would be if they were to learn that Walsh Camden was in a filthy dungeon in Mexico and that avarice had got him into that predicament.

16

The sun beat down, firecrackers exploded in the street, each report arousing a scurry of nervous hoofs among the livestock along the way. The snaredrummer in Otto Schneider's band, inspired by beer, burst into a long roll in Rezin Bartee's blacksmith shop. The bass drummer struck a booming, impatient note. Flies buzzed and babies wailed.

All Combabi awaited the pleasure of the Camdens. Always it had been the Camdens who chose the tune to which Combabi danced. But this time the fawners were going to be disappointed, Del believed. This time they were going to see their idol's feet of clay.

Even Lady Camden would not have the backbone to take part in a brass band parade now. Not after reading the message he had written with Juan Torreón's cigar sizzling on his flesh and Torreón's six-shooter lying on the table, pointed at his heart.

Here and there he began to hear sour grumbling among the tired bystanders. They had come here only to pay lip service. Under the surface they resented the Camdens. And feared them.

He laughed out loud, jeeringly. Faces turned with frowning question toward him. To him, their resentment of the delay appeared childish. It was founded on envy of the Camdens' on the resentment of the weak for the strong. None of them had ever been actually wronged by the Camdens, no doubt, other than being patronized.

They had no real desire to crush the Camdens, to smash them into the earth and humble their pride. Not as Del did.

A flurry of activity began in the hotel lobby. Harriet Camden and her niece appeared, escorted by the mayor and his committee. Del had underestimated Lady Camden's strength of will.

17

The group halted on the hotel steps and posed for a photographer who had set up his tripod and big blackhooded camera. The word went up and down Jefferson Street. The Camdens were ready. The procession could now get under way.

A cannon emitted a salute, the concussion hard and solid. The drums of Otto Schneider's Silver Comet Band rolled into a march step, and the bandsmen swung into view up the street.

Harriet Camden and her niece, managing the trains of their gowns, were assisted into the barouche. Lady Camden's gray eyes touched on Del briefly where he stood leaning against the wall of the hotel, rods away. Her glance was cool and self-assured. It carried a command. A command, not a request. That was the Camden way.

He knew as clearly as though she had spoken, that she was ordering him to say nothing about the message he had brought from Juan Torreón. Her eyes turned away as she seated herself in the carriage, arranging her skirts.

Kay Camden had also singled him out. But he understood that this was in spite of herself, for she had discovered his presence by accident and had been unable to avoid giving him a second look. A look of challenge, and, like that of her aunt's, a command.

Mayor Donally joined them in the barouche, taking a seat facing to the rear, along with Martin Osborne the manager of the Aurora Mercantile. The coachman gazed over his shoulder at the color bearers and the band up the street, awaiting their approach so that he could swing the carriage into line.

But there was a delay. The ornate saddles of the twopalominos remained empty. Heads craned this way and that, searching for the two missing riders.

18

"Them cussed Camden boys air always late," a bystander snorted. "Theyll be likkered up as usual when they show up—if'n they doshow up."

Messengers raced away. The band and the parade marked time. Presently Cullen Camden appeared and came swaggering to mount one of the palominos.

He blew a kiss in the direction from which he had come, then bowed with exaggerated deference to his mother. He was drunk. He hooked a knee over the horn while he waited for his brother. He scanned the crowd, giving particular attention to any comely females within reach of his smirk and his wink.

Then he discovered Del in the background. He sat straighter. "Damned if we haven't got a border hopper among us," he said loudly.

At that moment his older brother came pushing through the crowd and leaped aboard the second palomino. Quinn Camden was a big man with Indian-black hair and milky gray eyes. No razor could ever entirely whiten his jaws. He was powerful of shoulder, box-jawed, lean-waisted, and palpably in top physical condition.

Quinn was three years older than either Cullen or Del. Both the Camden brothers, as youngsters, had been sent to military schools, for the discipline it would offer. It had been with indifferent results. Quinn was a person who lived to fight with his fists. He had fought in the ring, in fact, although his parents had tried to keep that quiet.

Not that Quinn had needed money. He had fought because it had given him the chance to bruise flesh and maim features with his hands. He had a natural talent for it, both for the maiming and the art of boxing. No man in the Combabi had ever taken his measure in a fist battle, and it had been a long time since anyone had the temerity to attempt it.

Quinn had even had the confidence to spar with James J. Corbett when Gentleman Jim appeared in Combabi on an exhibition tour. He had also traveled to El Paso to test his skill against Bob Fitzsimmons under similar circumstances. He had been knocked out on both occasions, but had been far from disgraced.

He had been drinking also, but he had always been better able to carry his liquor than his brother. Del noticed as Quinn swung into the saddle that he might have put on a few pounds in these past half a dozen years, but there was still the old sinewy grace in his posture.

Cullen spoke to him and Quinn twisted around to search out Del among the crowd. Del stood with a thumb hooked in his belt, smiling a little and let Quinn size him up.

He and Quinn had fought on three occasions as boys. That was the exact number. Three. Del would never forget. He could still remember those beatings. For Quinn had been older, bigger, and heavier. He had never been one to spare an opponent, even as a boy.

Quinn said something to his brother and they both laughed loudly. Ed Donally waved his silk hat as a signal, and the Silver Comet Band swung into step and struck up a tune. It came blaring past. Quinn and Cullen gigged their horses. The palominos, shadow-dancing, their pale manes and tails flying, pranced into line. The barouche swung into motion and followed them down Jefferson Street.

Lady Camden was smiling brightly, nodding to the onlookers. She was the picture of refined self-possession, apparently without a thought on her mind beyond the enjoyment of the day.

Del watched, a knowledge of defeat in him. He even had to admire Harriet Camden for the way she was upholding the family tradition. As far as the spectators were concerned, all was right with the world and with the Camdens.

However, Kay Camden was not as adept at mastering her real emotions. She also was attempting to smile and bob her head, but the smile was only pasted on her lips, which were stiff and pale.

At least he had seen beneath the surface of the Camdens and knew that their armor could be pierced. He tried to find some satisfaction in that—and failed. He walked up the street toward the livery. The tail of the procession passed by. The sidewalk ahead became deserted as the spectators fled to shelter from the scorching sun.

As he passed the wide door of Rezin Bartee's blacksmith shop, where the beer keg still stood in its tub of ice, he saw from the corner of an eye the burly, oaken-shouldered man with the short black beard who had been host to the bandsmen.

He kept moving onward, but the smithy spoke in a deep voice. "Come in here, drat your hide."

Del hesitated, then entered the shop. The forge fire was cold, the anvil silent. The smithy had on his rusty black Sunday suit, white shirt and celluloid collar which he donned only an special occasions and on the Sabbath when he sang in the Baptist Church choir.

The interior of the grimy, rickety building, with its high peaked roof and dirt floor, was cool and dim. Del drew a deep breath into his lungs. "There's nothing in the world that smells as clean as a smith's shop," he said.

The bearded man held a stone mug under the spigot and coaxed it to fill from the nearly empty keg.

"Here's to you, Rezin," Del said and tilted the mug. The beer was cold, and he drank deep and thirstily.

"And there's nothing that does the work better than iced beer on a July day in Combabi," he said.

They shook hands. "You shouldn't do this, Rezin," Del said.

"It'll be a sorry day when a man can't speak to such as he chooses," Rezin Bartee snorted.

"They might add two, and two together," Del said.

"Let 'em. There're some things I've done, in my life that I wished I hadn't. But ridin' with Dave Kittridge ain't one of 'em. I'd do it agin, if it come that way."

"You better not let the Camdens hear you talk like that."

Rezin shrugged. "I'm mighty near sure for certain that Walsh Camden knew I was a Long Rider."

"I doubt that. Otherwise, you'd have been roughed out of the Combabi long ago. Or worse."

"Maybe. But it wasn't me that Walsh Camden wanted. It was your father he holds responsible for what's happened to Two Star. He blames a dead man."

"What do you mean? What's happened to Two Star?"

Rezin eyed him. "How long have you been away, Del?"

"Going on six years."

"Soldierin' all that time?"

"No. I fought in Cuba and the Philippines, but when I was mustered out I threw in at first with an American prospector down in Sonora who said he had something good to follow up. It was in the Ladrone Mountains, a wild place. We worked there for six months, driving a shaft, for it was a silver trace in quartz that we were

22

following."

"I've mined," Rezin said. "It's work. Bitter work."

"We must have moved a thousand tons of *borrasca* before we got into bonanza ore," Del said. "Then the military governor, who was only a grafter and a thief, moved in, had us arrested on trumped-up charges and seized the mine. His *soldados* gave us the *ley de fuga,* the law of flight, to give them an excuse to shoot us down. I made it, with a bullet in me. My partner, Tug Johnson, didn't."

"I knew Tug," Rezin said. "A good man."

"After that I rode for an American-owned cattle outfit in Chihuahua. *Políticos* grafted all the profits. Finally a bunch of cutthroats who called themselves liberators killed the owners and half of the vaqueros, including a lot of fine Mexicans. They burned the rancho and ran off with all the cattle and horses they could handle."

Del finished the beer in the mug. "That sort of thing was going on all over northern Mexico. And still is. I threw in with Juan Torreón. He had just come into prominence. He had been a vaquero himself. At first he fought for the people who were being robbed by the kind I just mentioned. He was a liberator. *Viva libertad! Viva Mejico! Viva Torreón!*"

"That's the way they all start," Rezin said grimly.

Del nodded. "He went the way of the other liberators. He got the taste of power. And of gold. He wasn't a liberator any longer. He was just a bandit who looted and pillaged. I turned against him. I had been a *capitán* in his army. I joined with other patriotic Mexicans and was trying to organize a force big enough to smash him when one of our *compañeros* proved to be a traitor and trapped us into Torreón's hands. I was to be shot."

"I was told you were dead," Rezin said.

"You seem to keep in touch with things," Del said.

"Many men drift into blacksmith shops," Rezin said. "From everywhere. Even from across the line. Border hoppin' didn't end when Dave Kittridge was killed. And that answers your question about what's happened to Two Star."

"I don't follow you."

"Your father showed how it could be done," Rezin said. "He set out to take from Two Star only what Walsh Camden had taken from him and other men. Since then there's been others who just take. Star has been rustled an' border-jumped by men your father wouldn't even spit on. Now that the Army's moved in to patrol the line, it don't pay to hop cattle any longer. It means a long jolt in a federal prison. But it came too late. Star looks as big as ever—in size. So does a skeleton. The Camdens are about busted."

"Busted?" Del said skeptically. "I should be that broke. They still ride in fancy buggies and on silver saddles."

"They're puttin' up a front. Not too many folks know they're on their uppers. But the ones who count know it. Fact is, some of 'em joined in pickin' the bones. Such as Ed Donally. He owns the bank now, not Walsh Camden. Other people own the Sun House. That was Walsh's pride. His red apple. He designed it, built it with his own money. The Camdens don't even own the barouche they're paradin' in, nor them two show saddles. I own 'em. I loan it to the Camdens for the sake of old times, and for appearance. I figure I owe it to Harriet Camden to help keep her chin high, bein' as I was the one that helped bust Two Star. I hold no grudge ag'in Harriet."

Del was staring disbelievingly.

Rezin nodded. "That's the way it is. The Camdens

have been rustled, slow-elked, border-hopped, brand-blotted, sleepered an' just plain stole from until they don't even bother to renew grazin' leases. Even their own cowboys steal from 'em, such as are left on the payroll."

"And my father started all this?"

"The buzzards always move in after the he-wolf leaves. About the only real asset Walsh Camden has left is his horse range an' that strain of saddlestock that he's developed at Star. The market for horseflesh is mighty thin, what with electric street cars an' all them other new doofangles they're buildin' back East. There's no demand even for Camden horses."

"Except across the line."

Rezin shrugged. "Maybe you haven't heard, but Uncle Sam says no. It used to be that a border hopper had only the Rangers to worry about. If he got caught, there weren't many juries in these parts that would convict him. Most of the jurors had run the line themselves at one time or other. It's different now. It means ten years or more in a federal jug if you're caught runnin' anything south. The cavalry rides every inch o' the line, day an' night."

Del thoughtfully rolled a cigarette. He scraped the tobacco from the bottom of the small cotton sack. It was of poor quality at best and so dry and flaky he had to be patient in the task in order to treasure every scrap.

If Walsh Camden was willing to take a chance on going to prison by selling contraband. horses, what Rezin had said about the low ebb of the Camden fortunes apparently was not only true but understated. Two Star must be in desperate circumstances indeed, for its owner to have risked Torreón's wrath by trying to sell his horses at a higher price to a rival *insurrecto*.

25

Del lighted his smoke from a match that Rezin held for him. Rezin watched him in silence. From the distance came the music of the bands. The parade was entering the rodeo grounds on the far side of town where it would disband.

"You talked to Harriet Camden," Rezin finally said. "I saw you go to Sun House. I saw the way that purty Kay Camden glared at you when she come out to get into the carriage. Everybody's wonderin' why Walsh Camden wasn't in the parade. The Camdens say he's under the weather. But I happen to know he ain't been at the ranch for a couple o' weeks. You know somethin', don't you?"

"It could be something you'd wish you didn't know, if I told you," Del said. He changed the subject. "What about the place? Rafter K?"

Rezin frowned. "You'd likely not even know where it had stood."

"I'll know."

"Walsh Camden wiped out everything. He burned the buildings. Pulled even the corral bars into the fire. Sent in field hands with ox teams and plows an' scrapers. They buried even the ashes an' the foundation rocks. Brush has moved in. The last time I rode by, I couldn't tell just where the spread had stood."

"I'll know," Del repeated. "I'll rebuild it. Just as it had been. And on just where it had stood."

Rezin was startled. "Hold on! Walsh Camden will—!"

"Where it stood is still my land," Del said. "I've seen to it that the taxes were kept paid. I made sure the Camdens would never get their hands on that land. Walsh Camden kept trying. He tried to have the section sold for taxes more than once."

26

"He likely knowed you'd come back sometime."

"And now I'm back."

"I've seen feuds an' grudges," Rezin said, "but I've never seen nothin' like it was between Walsh Camden an' Dave Kittridge. The bitterness. It scared me. Walsh was like a man possessed of the devil. It went beyond greed for money or range. It was somethin' in his soul. Del, let a man who rode with your father an' saw this ugly thing give you a word of advice."

"I know what it'll be," Del said. "It's no use, Rezin. I'm staying. I'm not coming back with a gun in my hand. Nor to stir up old grudges. I'm not on the kill. But I'll let no Camden haze me around."

Rezin spread his hands in a gesture of defeat. After a moment, he asked quietly: "How are you fixed for money, Del?"

Del thought of what he had in his pocket. Some six silver American dollars and a few pieces of small change. That, along with his horse and saddle and the clothes on his back, was all that he had brought with him across the border after those years in Mexico. And he had been furnished even with these by Juan Torreón who wanted to make sure he would be able to carry out his mission to Combabi.

"I'm in good shape," he said.

They again shook hands. "I'll see you later, Rezin," he said.

It had been his intention to get his horse and leave town. Now, he decided to put it off, for that day at least.

He ate a cheap meal in a hashhouse, then located a shabby, backstreet hotel that catered to unshaven, taciturn, sun-dried men, such as he, who came out of the depths of the land, lingered a day or a week, and disappeared back into that vacuum with no questions

27

asked—or answered.

The slatternly landlady showed no sign of recognizing his name when he signed the dog-eared book. The price for the night was a dollar, in advance. He paid an extra two bits for towels and hot water and a tub.

He gave the woman another dollar for a shirt, socks, and underwear that he selected from items she had on hand to supply the needs of guests. They were not new, but they were at least clean and ironed.

He shaved, bathed, then slept soundly for three hours, despite the heat in the room. Awakening, he dressed, and felt better able to cope with Combabi town.

CHAPTER 3

THE SOLID HEAT OF MIDAFTERNOON LAY ON THE TOWN when he emerged. The customary barbecue was in progress at the rodeo grounds where the parade had ended long since. There a man could eat his fill for a quarter.

Del entered the cottonwood-shaded picnic grounds, his hat tilted far back on his head so they all would know with whom they were dining Charlie Parker, who was in charge of collections, started to refuse his money, then took a second look at Del's dark eyes and decided otherwise.

But Del ate alone at a wooden table. The half-dozen other diners, who were strangers to him, became self-conscious at the way attention had centered on that table and had moved elsewhere with their half-finished plates.

A ragtag wagon carnival had pitched tents on the grounds to offer entertainment over the holiday. Barkers were extolling the wonders of the sideshows and games of skill and the delights of watching the gyrations of dancing girls. The hurdy-gurdy on a merry-go-round blared out mechanical tunes.

Del had three dollars and the small change in his pocket. As he ate he tried to puzzle out a way of improving his financial situation.

He listened to the bullfrog voice of a barker at one of the carnival attractions. He could see the faded red and yellow banner that portrayed a boxing bout.

"The next champion of the world, ladies and gentlemen," the barker was repeating. "We are prohibited from revealing the real identity of the Masked Marvel because of contract agreements with future opponents, one of whom will be the champion himself."

The pitch continued. Del had heard it in the past in essentially the same words. Every traveling carnival company in cattle country had its boxing show on its midway and its Masked Marvel or its Hooded Wonder. The boxing show was a major attraction for riders and ranchers because after the usual bouts between paid members of the show's crew a free-for-all challenge was invariably issued by the masked pugilist to any opponent who chose to step forward and try his prowess in the ring.

"In gold money," the barker was saying. "To any man who can stay in the ring with the Masked Marvel for two rounds we will pay twenty dollars. For three rounds the reward will be thirty dollars. Cash money, gentlemen, far a few minutes of exercise. For four rounds—the sum of fifty dollars. And . . ."

The barker paused for dramatic effect.". . . and, hear this, my friends. We will pay the sum of two hundred

29

dollars to anyone who defeats the Marvel, either by a decision or a knockout."

Del finished his food and walked in that direction. He joined the fringe of the crowd. The majority were men from the ranches, along with a sprinkling of townspeople. There was ribald comment and horseplay, with friends making a show of pushing each other forward to challenge the Masked Marvel. But Del saw the shine in the eyes of many for action—the urge to see blood spilled.

There were usually young game cocks in any range country who prided themselves on their fistic ability and believed that, given the chance to attract the eye of experts, they would make their name and fortune in the ring as professionals. It was an untrained amateurs that itinerant pugilists like the Masked Marvel made their living.

The barker's pitch reached its climax. ". . . and now, ladies and gentlemen, let me present to you the future champion of the world. The Masked Marvel, my friends. In person."

The Masked Marvel appeared from the tent and vaulted to the platform. He had a vivid orange bathrobe draped over his shoulders and wore a white silk headpiece that came to his shoulders and had slits for seeing and breathing. He was taller than the barker by inches, and the barker, who had the earmarks of an ex-pugilist, was far from puny.

Del peered closer. A man who had sifted through the crowd to join him, touched his arm. The arrival was Rezin Bartee.

"Recognize him?" Rezin murmured.

"You mean I'm not seeing things?" Del said. "That *can't* be Quinn Camden?"

"Can an' is."

"With a leppie outfit like that? Quinn Camden?"

"You're seein' him with your own eyes, ain't you? It's Quinn, sure enough. The real Masked Marvel is a broken-down pug who can't stay away from the bottle. He went off on a bender when the show hit town yesterday, an' likely is somewhere sleepin' it off. Quinn took his place."

"The Camdens can't be that hard up."

"That might have somethin' to do with it, at that," Rezin said. "Quinn always was a free spender. It likely gravels him to be pinched in the pocketbook. But Quinn naturally likes to maul people with his fists."

"Yes," Del sad. "I remember." How well he remembered the beatings he had taken as a boy at Quinn Camden's hands.

"Quinn's got a mean streak in him as wide as his shoulders," Rezin said. "He's always tryin' to pick fights, but everybody around here knows they won't stand a chance. So they swallow his insults rather than be beat to a pulp. They all know he might have gone a long way as a fighter if his father would have stood for him turning pug. But Walsh Camden said he'd disown him if be disgraced the family by goin' into the ring."

"I see what you mean," Del said.

"Quinn jumped at the chance to wear a mask an' beat up some of these young cowpokes who don't know what they're up ag'in. Quinn put two boys in the hospital last night."

"Last night? You mean this is the second day he's been at this?"

"That's right. Lonnie Barnes, a nice young rider from up Red Lake way, took a shot at earnin' a little side money ag'in the Masked Marvel last night. Quinn cut

31

him to doll rags in two minutes. Worked on an eye an' the doctor says he's liable to lose the sight of it. Jaw broken, teeth knocked out. Some men never get over bein' brute-beat like that. The other boy didn't get off much better. Broken ribs, face looks like he was kicked by a mule."

"Didn't they know they were up against Quinn?"

"I reckon not. I didn't know it myself 'til just now. It ain't easy to see a man clear at night under the kerosene torches. I knew the pug who's the real Masked Marvel was on a drunk, for he slept in my shop last night, but I didn't know 'til now that it was Quinn who was takin' his place. I should have guessed it when I heard about how them two other boys had been laid up. I guess some folks will recognize him, now he's come out in daylight."

Del appraised the bystanders. He decided that few, if any, had identified Quinn Camden under the mask. However, three cowpunchers in town clothes, who stood together in the background, were grinning knowingly.

"Two Star riders," Rezin said. "They know it's Quinn."

Del discovered that Quinn Camden was gazing at him, his eyes malicious through the holes in the mask. It was a baiting challenge.

The barker ended his pitch and patrons began paying their half dollars and filing into the tent. Del moved forward.

Rezin grabbed his arm. "Hold on, Del! I saw the way you two looked at each other. I got a hunch that's why Quinn came out in the open. He knew you was out here and he made sure you'd recognize him. You ain't aimin' to do what I think's in your mind, are you?"

32

"I've waited a long time to grow up to Quinn's size," Del said.

"He'll slaughter you! He's good! Real good! Didn't I just tell you what happened to those other two—?"

"It'll have to be settled between us, sooner or later," Del said. "Right now, I've got a chance to get paid for it."

"You're broke, ain't you?" Rezin demanded. "Look! I've got some *dinero* laid away. Enough to—"

His offer died away. He sighed. "You damned Kittridges always was prouder'n Lucifer. Too proud to ask for help. Or take any."

"Money I might never be able to pay back," Del said. "In everything else the Kittridges, what's left of them, are already in your debt."

He moved into the ticket line. Quinn Camden waited to make sure Del was really intending to enter the tent. He lifted a hand in a mocking gesture, then leaped from the platform and vanished inside.

Rezin bought a ticket and followed Del into the tent. A shabby boxing ring was flanked by tiers of slat seats. The sun, beating down on the weathered top, shed a sickly yellow light. The interior was breathlessly hot although the skirts of the canvas walls. were raised for ventilation.

Del led the way to the seats and they settled down. Patrons continued to file in. The tent must have had a capacity of nearly two hundred and the seats were well-filled before the gravel voice of the barker finally ceased outside.

"Word of what happened to the other two boys has got around," Rezin said. "People don't want to miss the slaughter if any other sucker is fool enough to try it." He gave Del a dour side glance.

33

The jingle of spur chains and the drawl of cow country voices filled the tent, for many of the patrons were still in the colorful garb they had worn in the parade. Del was aware he was still a marked man and that he might be another of the reasons why attendance was so brisk.

The barker appeared and took the role of an announcer and referee. He introduced himself as Buck Golden and bawled out a flowery, mechanical speech and then presented two battle-scarred pugilists as opponents in the first bout.

This proved to be a boring three-round exhibition between men who fought with a great display of slapping gloves that did no damage and ended with the fake knockout of the one whose turn it was to go down.

A bag-punching display by the barker himself came next. Then Quinn Camden, in his role as the Masked Marvel, was introduced with a flourish and a trumpeting of the barker's voice.

"Three rounds of serious competition as part of the Masked Marvel's coming bouts with top men of the American prize ring," the barker boomed. "In this corner, gentlemen, the contender for the world's championship, who I must introduce only as the Masked Marvel. And in the opposite corner Bakersfield Jack, heavyweight champion of California."

Bakersfield Jack was a gnarled old-time fragment of driftwood an the grim seas of the prize ring. He had misshapen ears, scarcely anything that resembled a nose and eyes shadowed by masses of scar tissue.

Quinn Camden tossed aside his bathrobe. Five years had toughened and seasoned him. He was a fine physical specimen, evidently in top condition. Del heard an admiring murmur in the crowd.

34

Quinn, as he moved to the center of the ring, once more singled out Del for a mocking look. Then he touched gloves with Bakersfield Jack in the routine manner—and that was the only gesture that followed the usual procedure.

The spectators had settled back to watch with patience what they anticipated would be a repetition of the first staged bout. Soon they began to sit up, and lean forward with a growing mass sensation of disbelief.

Quinn's hands were darting like rapiers. The contact of his gloves was scarcely audible in contrast to the explosive exhibition of glove-slapping in the earlier offering.

The crowd's attitude changed from disbelief to shock. Here and there some eyes began to shine again with delight. But the main reaction was revulsion.

For blood was spurting. Quinn was boxing with cold precision. His gloves were tearing flesh and bringing gore. The battered face of the pugilist was taking punishment that must have been as vicious as any it had endured in the past. It was the more spine-chilling because it was being done with such impersonal violence.

The pug, surprised at first, became terrorized. He tried to defend himself, tried to protect his face from the swords that slashed him. He turned appealingly to the barker. That individual seemed stunned also, and made only a feeble, muttered protest to Quinn.

Quinn moved in all the more relentlessly. The pug, whimpering in complete terror, tried to escape by back-pedaling. Quinn followed him mercilessly and knocked him out with a right and a left that brought groans of protest from the spectators.

The battered man's head struck the unpadded floor of

the ring with a thud. He lay, arms outflung, as though paralyzed.

The barker and men of the crew brought water and worked frantically over him. Quinn strolled back to his comer, languidly pulled on his bathrobe and leaped over the ropes. He walked up the runway amid dead silence and vanished into the dressing quarters.

A stretcher was finally brought and Quinn's victim was carried away.

Del and Rezin looked at each other. "Quinn just can't help it," Rezin growled. "It's his pleasure."

After a long interval, while the uneasy silence held, the barker, Buck Golden, returned. He evidently had been shaken by the outcome of the match, but he was not letting that interfere with a day when box-office business was booming.

"And now, my friends," he intoned, "the Masked Marvel is ready to meet any challengers under the rules and rewards that we have announced. Here, my friends, is a chance to display your ability, to test your skill and prowess in the ring."

His voice droned on. "And now," he concluded, "will all challengers please come forward. You will all get your chance, gentlemen. One and all. In the order of your entrance in the list."

There was an uneasy stir and a nervous titter. No person arose. Buck Golden gazed around. "Come, come, my friends," he said scornfully. "Surely, you're not afraid. I expected a dozen of you husky young men to step forward. Why, last week, at El Paso, the Masked Marvel had so much opposition he was hard put. We paid out considerable money. Indeed we did. Surely, the Combabi country also grows men with sand in their craws."

36

Del stood up, shaking off Rezin's restraining hand. "Never mind about the sand in the craws," he said. "Your Masked Marvel's got a challenger."

He walked to ringside amid a startled rumble of voices. He held up an arm for silence. "The name's Kittridge," he said to Buck Golden. "Del Kittridge. If you haven't heard that name there are others here who have."

Absolute silence clapped down again for a moment. Buck Golden peered, a sudden wariness in his puffy face. He sensed that there were waters here whose depth he did not understand.

"Have you done any fighting, my friend?" he asked cautiously.

"Some," Del said.

Golden hesitated, then said, "Wait here."

He left the ring and went hurrying to the dressing quarters. Del knew he wanted to talk things over with Quinn Camden.

The conference was brief. Golden came hurrying back. He looked angry and at a loss as though he had been given a dressing down for causing delay. But he also seemed pleased that the decision had been made for him. He nodded to Del. "All right. Be ready in five minutes. Where are your togs?"

"Togs?" Then Del understood. "You mean ring clothes? I didn't bring any with me."

"We'll fix you up," Golden said. "Step lively. We've got more shows to do this afternoon."

He led Del to the dressing room and Rezin followed.

"Who's this fella?" Golden demanded, eying Rezin.

"I'm actin' as my friend's, second," Rezin said. "Any other questions?"

Golden took a second look at Rezin and decided he

37

had none. He fished faded boxing trunks and worn ring shoes from a trunk and tossed them on a camp stool. "They'll fit," he said.

Del ignored the trunks, but tried on the shoes. They were sizes too big and the flat soles were worn thin. They would offer treacherous footing. Even so, they were preferable to fighting in saddleboots or barefoot.

Del donned the shoes and stripped off his shirt. "This will do," he said.

"Suit yourself," Golden said. He brought out boxing gloves which he attempted to push on Del's hands.

Del brushed them aside. "Just a minute. What about the money?"

"Money?"

"I'm sure you've heard the word before. The twenty dollars for staying two rounds. Fifty for four rounds. And two hundred if your man loses."

Golden threw back his head and guffawed. "You'll git your money, fellow. If you earn it, that is."

"Sure," Del said. "But let's see the color of it. I want it tacked to a ring post so the crowd can watch it."

He flipped the back of his hand against Golden's flabby stomach. The man winced and gasped.

Quinn Camden, wearing his mask, stepped into the tent. Evidently he had been eavesdropping. "Get the cash and put it on a post, Buck," he said.

Buck Golden was unhappy. "Now, wait a minute, Camd—"

He caught himself and avoided finishing the name. He glared at Del. "Are you doubting our honesty?" he blustered.

Del laughed. "Yes."

Quinn Camden laughed, too. "Put it up, Buck," he said. "Don't worry. It'll be safe enough. Kittridge won't

38

collect."

"You seem to know this guy," Golden said.

"That," Quinn said, "is for sure."

Golden, scowling and reluctant, left and presently returned carrying a roll of greenbacks. He said surlily, "All right. Here it is."

"Count it, Rezin," Del said.

Golden tried to back away, but Rezin caught him by the arm and reached for the money. Golden resisted, intending to keep possession. His features began to contort as Rezin's grip tightened.

Del could sympathize with Golden. He had seen Rezin tear decks of cards in two with those fingers, seen him bend horseshoes into pretzel shape.

"Blast you!" Golden gasped, surrendering the bills.

Rezin counted the money. "You're forty dollars short," he said scornfully. "You measly, short-card sport, I've got a notion to spank you."

"Come up with it, Buck," Quinn Camden snapped impatiently. "Let's get started with this."

Golden sullenly delved in a pocket and counted out more bills. "All right," Del said. "Rezin, see to it they're placed on a ring post."

He pulled on the gloves Golden had furnished and let Rezin take care of the lacings.

Rezin frowned as he worked. "Twelve-ounce gloves, maybe heavier," he muttered. "These damned things are worse'n pillows."

Del turned to where Quinn had been standing, intending to compare gloves. But he had left the dressing room. The crowd began yelling in the main tent and Del knew Quinn was already entering the ring.

"No matter," he said. "Twelve ounces, twelve tons. I've waited for this too long to be bothered by ounces."

He walked into the arena and down the aisle to the ring where Quinn waited, the bathrobe around his shoulders. Rezin followed at his heels.

Buck Golden was nervous as he addressed the crowd. "The challenge match, gentlemen. In this corner the Masked Marvel, the future champion of the world. And in the opposite corner, the challenger whose name is Del Kittridge of—"

He turned to Del for information. "Of the border jumpers," Del said.

That brought a stir and a stamping of feet in the crowd. "You got gall, Kittridge," a cowboy yelled. "Standin' there bold as brass, admittin' you're a cattle thief."

"You've got things twisted," Del said. "A man can't steal what rightly belongs to him."

"Maybe you was a hero, fightin' the Filipinos," another yelled, "but yore only a long rider to us."

The two who had spoken were men Rezin had pointed out as riders for Two Star. Cullen Camden was sitting with them and Del knew he had coached the speakers.

The remainder of the onlookers preferred to remain just that. Onlookers.

CHAPTER 4

ROUND ONE!" BUCK GOLDEN BLARED UNEXPECTEDLY, and a bell clanged.

Del found Quinn upon him almost before he could lift his hands. He parried a right and took a glove on his forearm. It should have been a harmless impact but pain shot through his arm. He knew that Quinn was sure to

40

follow with a right cross. He faded away and this punch only grazed his side. Even so he felt the shock of bruised flesh.

He had been rushed off balance by the speed of Quinn's attack and he clenched. He was looking into Quinn's eyes through the opening in the mask. Quinn was laughing gleefully.

Del suddenly understood! The gloves Quinn wore were not boxing gloves. They were only coverings to hide tape and tinfoil that armed his fists and made clubs of them. Quinn was equipped with lethal weapons.

"I should have known," he said. "You Camdens never change, do you?"

"Break! Break!" Buck Golden tried to pry them apart, but it was Del's arms he sought to impede.

Del shoved Quinn away, then jostled Golden so that the man went staggering back and landed on his hip pockets.

Quinn came in again savagely Del crouched, ducked a right, stepped inside a left and drove a fist to Quinn's stomach.

"Foul! Foul!" Golden yelled, climbing to his feet.

Rezin Bartee rose like a bear alongside the ring, climbed through the ropes, seized Golden and lifted him with effortless might and dropped him soggily out of the enclosure.

"That was no foul," Rezin roared. "I'll referee this fight. Square an' honest."

They all knew the blacksmith. No objection was raised. Quinn Camden did not bother to press the claim of foul. That punch had shaken him, however, taught him caution. He was suddenly aware that in weight and strength he no longer had the advantage of their boyhood days.

41

His hesitation was momentary. In the next instant he was driving in again, his stamina unimpaired.

Del knew that if he was squarely hit by those loaded gloves he was done for. The best he could hope to get out of it would be to be knocked out. He began moving, feinting, side-stepping and backing away. Quinn missed with a right, was short with a left.

Del caught Quinn flush on the jaw with a right, jolting him. Quinn shook that off and came in, trying to crowd Del into a corner and set him up for a smash.

Del faded away, ducking a vicious left jab. He was aware of a new disadvantage. The ring shoes Buck Golden had given him were as great a liability as the pillow boxing gloves. The soles were so slick they gave him no purchase on the canvas.

A fist caught him just below the belt with the impact of a sledge. He heard Rezin's voice, dim and far away. "Where's the timekeeper? Where'n blazes is the bell? This round must be over!"

There was no bell. Del knew there never would be a bell as long as Quinn wanted to continue fighting.

Quinn was on him, measuring him and dealing punishment. He felt the weight of the blows. He rammed a fist into Quinn's throat and Quinn gave ground. He launched a left and it landed on the jaw. But he realized there was no strength in it.

He saw Quinn's right coming toward his body. It was as though he was a spectator instead of a participant. Time and movement seemed to have slowed. He had the impression that he and Quinn were battling in murky water, with their actions sluggish and mechanical.

Quinn's mailed glove seemed to float against him and strike over the heart. His own right fist again made contact with Quinn's jaw at the same time. This time he

42

felt the solid jar of the impact run up his arm. He was aware of vague, surprised satisfaction.

After that he didn't know anything, although he had wild dreams and distorted thoughts.

He found himself, at last, staring up into Rezin's face. "I've seen you some place before," he mumbled.

"You're lucky you can see me now," Rezin said. "I thought you were a goner."

Gradually, Del discovered he was lying on a cot in the dressing quarters. Alongside Rezin was a man he recognized. He was Dr. Abraham Samuelson, small, graying, and kindly, who had served the medical needs of the Combabi country since before Del was born. It was Doc Abe who had helped bring him into the world.

"I'm supposed to ask what happened," Del said. "I already know. Apparently I didn't even make it through the first round against Quinn."

"Round!" Rezin snorted. "Five minutes or more. It was my fault. I should have savvied they'd long-round us in addition to pulling every other dirty trick in the bag."

Doc Abe counted Del's pulse. The glow of daylight on the canvas top was turning crimson. The hurdy-gurdy on the merry-go-round had a tired sound. The holiday was ending. Sundown was at hand.

"Quinn must have put my lights out for quite a spell," Del mumbled.

"For keeps, almost," Rezin said. "You can thank your stars Doc Abe was handy."

Del puzzled over that. "I saw that punch coming," he said. "So slow. So slow. But I didn't feel myself going down."

"You were already out," Doc Abe said. "Out an your feet. Then you were hit over the heart. For a while it

43

was touch and go as to whether it would start going again."

"Hit with a glove loaded with tinfoil and water-soaked bandages and who knows what else," Rezin growled.

"Yeah," Del said. "I found that out right at the start."

"We can't prove it. Quinn got back on his feet and rabbited away before I could check up on his gloves. I was too worried about you right at that moment to chase him."

"What do you mean about Quinn getting back on his feet?" Del asked.

"You landed with a right to the jaw just as he gave you that punch to the heart," Rezin said. "I never saw two big men fall so fast. But you stayed down. Quinn managed to get up. But he'll have a sore jaw, I tell you."

Del tried to sit up but Doc Abe pushed him back.

"Easy, David," he cautioned. "I think you'll be all right, but give that pump a little more time to steady down."

Del sank back. "I was wrong a while ago, Doctor," he said. "I told Maggie Riley she was the only person in the world who still called me by my front handle."

Doc Abe smiled. "Who has a better right? I was not only there when you were born, but I was present when you were baptized. You can give thanks you inherited a strong constitution from your father and mother."

Del took stock of himself and became aware he had suffered considerable damage. He found it painful to move his left arm. He gingerly touched his face and discovered court plaster. His left eye was swollen almost shut.

"You'll hurt for a day or two," Doc Abe said. "But no bones are broken, as best I can find out. You'll know for

44

sure after you get moving around."

"Quinn might as well have used a cleaver," Rezin said. "I blame myself. I ought never to have let you go in there with him without takin' a look at his gloves."

"The Camdens always fought with loaded gloves," Del said. "It was my fault for not remembering."

He became aware that Doc Abe was trying to warn him to quit talking. A new arrival had entered the tent. He lifted his head.

Kathryn Camden stood in the entrance. She had, changed from the pretentious gown and flower arrangement that she had worn in the parade to a white blouse and skirt and a small straw bonnet.

"I heard that," she said.

"They say eavesdroppers never hear anything good of themselves," Del said.

"Aunt Harriet wants to talk to you," she said. "At once."

"At once?" Del asked caustically. "Dressed like this?"

"Certainly not," she said. "But come as soon as possible. We've been trying to locate you all afternoon."

"You must have looked in all the wrong places," Del said. "And here I was, all the time, being punched around by your cousin."

She moved closer, inspecting him. "You've been fighting!"

"And got licked."

"Did you and Quinn fight?"

"You might call it that. He had clubs. I had feather pillows."

"Are you hurt?"

"Mainly in the pocketbook. I still feel that Quinn owes me two hundred dollars."

45

"For what?"

"I doubt if you'd care to hear the details—or believe what I told you."

"If Quinn actually owes you any money, you'll be paid," she said.

"Sure," Del said. "The Camdens have a reputation for paying debts. Money—and otherwise."

Her mouth was a tight line. She had an explosive temper and was holding it in check with an effort. She turned to leave. "We'll expect you at Sun House immediately," she said icily.

"Have a nice, long wait," Del said.

She gave him a little, twisted smile. "You'll be there," she said. Then she left the tent.

Del sat up, despite Doc Abe's protests. He sat with his bare feet on the dusty earth, staring frowningly at the canvas flap that was still vibrating after Kay Camden's departure. He had an uneasy hunch that she also had come equipped with loaded gloves. She had been entirely too sure of herself, sure that she held the whiphand over him.

He finally got to his feet. He was shaky for a time, but presently he steadied. The paralyzing effects of the punch to the heart were fading.

Doc Abe listened to his heart and peered into his eyes. "That's better," he said with satisfaction. "You're out of it now. But you ought to take it easy for a day or two."

"Thanks," Del said. "What do I owe you?"

Doc Abe started to shrug it off, then saw the look in Del's face. "Two dollars," he said. He added dryly, "I should have known better. You Kittridges and your damned pride."

Del found his shirt and boots and socks and dressed.

46

He fished two dollars from his pocket and handed them to the doctor. "Saving a man's life comes cheap," he said.

"The real difficulty is in keeping them alive afterward," Doc Abe said. "It's hard on the nerves of their friends."

"That's a warning, I take it," Del said. "But, in spite of my ruckus with Quinn just now, I didn't carry a chip on my shoulder in coming back to Combabi. Not against the Camdens. Not against anyone. All I ask is to be left alone."

Doc Abe sighed. "Remember one thing, David. I'm not the only friend you have in the Combabi. Nor is Rezin. There are a lot of persons who think your father was a fine man."

He picked up his black bag in his quick, birdlike manner and left the tent.

The last glow of the sun faded from the canvas top. Del and Rezin walked into the deserted arena and out of the tent. The hurdy-gurdy was silent. Tents were already being struck along the midway.

"Speaking of friends," Rezin said. "What are they for? Nobody but a mule-headed Kittridge would try to make himself a stake the way you just did. I tell you I'm fixed so that I can lend you any—"

"I've still got money," Del said. He had a lone silver dollar and some small change in his pocket.

The brief, hot twilight was deepening as they walked up Jefferson Street. Lamps glowed in the windows of the Camden suite in Sun House. Del wondered if Harriet Camden was sitting there, calm and aristocratic, waiting for him to appear, sure that he would obey.

"You're continuing to make yourself conspicuous by associating with a Kittridge," Del said. "Everybody will

47

be sure you were a Long Rider."

"Let 'em," Rezin said. "Let 'em. An' be damned to 'em."

A man came hurrying from across the street. "Rezin!" he called. "Been lookin' fer you. My near wheeler has gone an' throwed a shoe. He's that Percheron with the quarter crack that you fixed up with that cross-plate job. I don't like to ask a man to work on a holiday, but I got a steam boiler to freight up to the Consolidated mine in the Emeralds, startin' first thing in the mornin', an' you're the only man who kin fix up that hawss."

"Sure, Jess," Rezin said. "Be right with you." He said to Del, "An' be damned to the Camdens." Then he went hurrying with the worried freighter toward his blacksmith shop down the street.

Del stood alone, gazing after Rezin's blocky figure. His gaze turned to the lighted windows in Sun House. He produced his lone dollar and flipped it from palm to palm, smiling wryly. Pride. Pride that forbade accepting a loan from Rezin.

False pride, perhaps. Proud men. High pride. That had been the cause of it. That was what he believed. But he did not know for certain.

He was only sure that, whatever had aroused the relentless enmity between his father and Walsh Camden, it had nothing to do with money or land or cattle, although on the surface that had apparently been the issue between them. It had brought financial ruin for Dave Kittridge and had made him an outlaw. It had sent Del's mother to her grave when she was still in the prime of life—broken by the strain and violence of the feud and by being told there was a price on the head of her husband.

The only land whose title remained in the Kittridge

48

name was the original section below Castle Dome on which Del had continued to pay taxes. He had not set foot on it, nor seen it in nearly six years.

That section had been the nucleus of the once-prosperous cattle outfit his father had built up by leasing graze and buying rights to strategic sections that commanded water holes and windmill tanks in a land where water was precious.

Del had been about sixteen when he first realized that Walsh Camden had become his father's bitter enemy. Before that, they had been close friends—or at least as close as any could be with Walsh Camden. He had always been an aloof man, hard to know, who sat apart from others. Even from his wife and sons. A proud, self-centered person.

Del, from childhood, had rather pitied Quinn and Cullen. Despite all the spotted ponies and fancy saddles that their father had given them from the time they were able to walk, despite all the private tutors that had been brought in because Walsh Camden had decided that the rangeland school was not good enough for his sons, it had seemed to Del they had so little where he had so much.

From childhood, he also had mounts to ride, and saddles to straddle. True, his steeds had not been the fancy, imported Shetlands that Walsh Camden had brought in for his sons. His saddles usually had been sacks of grain or straw tied across the backs of mares and colts.

As they grew into lank, brash ranch kids, Quinn and Cullen rode smart cutting horses on roundup and gaudy palominos, like those in the parade, when they appeared in town. Del had patched hand-me-down stock saddles aboard unpredictable cow ponies that had plenty of spook in them. When not in school, he had ridden out each morning with the crew for the day's work, come blizzard, come fair weather.

Quinn and Cullen, too, had been trained in ranch work, but with a difference. They had always been accompanied by someone their father had assigned to watch over them and keep them out of danger—and to report every wrong move they made. Every mistake.

Always they had been under Walsh Camden's iron thumb. The outcome was that when they grew to manhood they went wild, scorning all restraint. Quinn became the arrogant, fist-hungry bully, seeking victims on which to display his fighting skill. Cullen spent the biggest part of his time in dancehalls and saloons.

But the real difference had been Walsh Camden himself. He had ridden the range alone, aloof from the riders he hired, aloof even from his sons. Austere, dominant. Del had been told by his father that Walsh Camden, in his younger days, had been as fast with a rope and pigging string at the branding fires as any rider alive, and that he could pop brush and rope ladinos—the wild mavericks of the thickets, with the best of them.

But somewhere along the line he had become a man of black moods. Proud, silent, unapproachable. Scornful of weakness in others, he had become implacable in business dealings, ruthless toward even men who had considered him to be their friend.

Because he controlled the bank, which had been the financial pillar of the Combabi, he had held a club over many ranchers—including Dave Kittridge. He had wielded that club ruthlessly. His Two Star had absorbed first one small outfit, then another.

But it was Dave Kittridge, above all, that he went after. Every move he made, ostensibly against other

50

men, was really aimed at encirclement of the Kittridge Rafter K.

Dave Kittridge did not awaken to his predicament until too late. The day came when Rafter K found itself hemmed in by Two Star fences, cut off from access to Combabi Creek and from the tanks and water holes that made the upper range and benches feasible for stock raising.

At first, Del's father could not believe it. Why, he and Walsh Camden had shared blankets in the early days when Geronimo was raiding down from the upper country and hitting the thin settlements along the border. As young ranchers, they had courted the two belles in the Combabi. Their marriages had taken place only a month apart.

Their wives had been close friends. But, like the two men, they had drifted apart. The coldness that was to end in a bitter feud had been a creeping, glacierlike thing.

CHAPTER 5

DEL FELT THE CHILL OF THAT GLACIER ON HIM NOW AS he stood watching the lighted windows in Sun House. He remembered how it had crushed the life from his mother. He had seen the tragedy of it in her, as though she knew the real reason why Walsh Camden had suddenly set out to ruin them.

Walsh Camden had succeeded in that purpose. Del's father, once he realized he was caught in the python-grip of Two Star, fought back as desperately as a strong man of stubborn determination could fight.

But he was trapped. Eventually, all that he had to

show for his fifty years of life was the title to the section on which he had built the ranchhouse into which he had carried his bride thirty years in the past. That and the grave of that bride, who had faded away along with the ranch, as though both had shared the same life blood.

Dave Kittridge had become a border runner. A Long Rider. It was Two Star on which he preyed exclusively. He had gathered about him a band of men as determined as himself. The identity of the other members of the Long Riders had never been established, but it was whispered that few or none of them were strangers to Walsh Camden if he met them face to face, and that Dave Kittridge was not the only man who had felt the iron hand of Two Star and was fighting back.

It was understood that Walsh Camden had placed a price of five thousand dollars on Dave Kittridge—dead or alive. Because the law in Combabi County prohibited private citizens from offering rewards for wanted men, word of the bounty offer on the leader of the Long Riders was passed along from ear to ear.

As the Long Riders continued to run the border it was understood that Walsh Camden had increased the offer to ten thousand dollars. In gold.

That eventually brought results. Dave Kittridge slept now alongside his wife in his grave. Del had found his father lying at the door of their ranchhouse one morning, a bullet in his back. Dave Kittridge evidently had been shot miles away and hours earlier, and had managed to stay in the saddle until his horse had brought him home.

He had still been alive, but too far gone to more than mumble a word or two. He had died before he could make Del understand, but Del was sure his father had been trying to tell him the name of the man who had shot him.

It was accepted in the Combabi that the ten-thousand-dollar reward had been claimed. But nobody knew to whom Walsh Camden had paid the money. Therewere some who suspected it had never been paid, for the reason that it had been Camden himself who.had put that bullet in Dave Kittridge's back.

They were wrong. Del was sure the name his father had been trying to utter was not that of Walsh Camden. He had gone to great pains to check on Camden's whereabouts the night his father had been shot. He was convinced it could not have been the Two Star owner who had pulled the trigger.

But, along with everyone in the Combabi, he was equally sure it had been Camden money that had been responsible for firing the shot. The difference was microscopic. Dave Kittridge had been slain for the reward.

Del, contrary to general belief, had never taken part in his father's border running. He was labeled as one of the Long Riders, but he had never known the identity of any of his father's companions, with the exception of Rezin Bartee, and it had been by putting two and two together that he had become sure Rezin had been one of them.

"The law calls us rustlers," his father had told him. "We don't look at it that way, but it's best that you stay clear of us. We figure that Walsh Camden built himself up by tearin' us down. He did it the worst possible way—by betrayin' friends for his own gain. The cattle we run across the line really would belong to us, except for him. God knows, we get little enough for cattle down there. We take our risks. But you're of another generation. I don't want you to inherit this grudge from me. I want no taint of bitterness in anything I leave to

53

you. That's why I'll never let you ride with us."

Del vanished into Mexico a few days after his father's funeral. Walsh Camden began to breathe easier, believing he had seen the last of the Long Riders. But the rustling was resumed, and on a scale greater than before. Two Star beef began vanishing in driblets and by the score.

The cattle disappeared into the soft featherbed that was Mexico, where the questions of pursuing gringo cattlemen were not clearly understood by the peons, and what information they offered led Walsh Camden and his men into blind trails. Intricate brands blotted out the Two Star iron on cattle that Walsh Camden knew were really his. These were the indecipherable *quién sabe* brands of Mexico. Who knows their meaning?

Then came the run that was to be known in the Combabi as the Big Raid. Nearly a thousand head of prime Two Star beef vanished into Mexico just before beef roundup. There was no question but what the members of Dave Kittridge's Long Riders were responsible and that they had planned and carried out the huge run as a sort of memorial to their dead leader.

Del had heard about the Big Raid long after it had taken place and that it had been a staggering blow to Two Star.

He had also heard that it was again whispered that there was bounty money being offered on a Kittridge, and that this time it was himself that Walsh Camden wanted, dead or alive.

The truth was that Del had not even been in Mexico at the time. The Spanish-American War had broken out shortly after his father's death and he had headed for a recruiting office at El Paso.

He had intended to join the Rough Riders, but their

ranks were filled before he could make it to El Paso. For the sake of quick action he joined the U. S. 4th Infantry and was soon in a training camp at Tampa, Florida. It was there that he had heard about the Big Raid.

He had fought in Cuba, and then had gone through the bloody Aguinaldo campaign in the Philippines with the 4th Infantry.

He was thinking of those days as he stood, absently watching shadows move on the curtained windows of the Camden suite across the narrow street. One shadow seemed to be that of a man. Del watched it with only a small part of his mind as he thought of the past—and of the future.

He was thinking that it might have been a mistake to come back to the Combabi. Nothing had changed. Not really. The pettiness, the hidden intrigues, the thirst for scandal were still here. And the intolerance. He was labeled as a cattle thief. A Long Rider.

He thought of other things. Of charging up El Caney hill with the 4th, under fire from Spanish troops in a blockhouse. He remembered the heat, the steaming tropical heat and the heavy blue uniforms they had been issued. He remembered the bullet that had struck him in the side, and how he had continued the charge up the hill.

He recalled the Philippines and a place called Bloody Bend near a *barrio* named Bacoor in the jungle where he had also fought and bled. After Aguinaldo surrendered and he had been mustered out, he had returned to Mexico and had joined in the disastrous silver-mining venture that had eventually impelled him to join Juan Torreón's false cause of liberation.

He suddenly came to attention. The shadow on the window had crystallized, become sharp and distinct.

55

The man had moved very close to the window. There was also the shadow of a woman to whom he seemed to be talking. Lady Camden.

Details were impossible to make out at that distance. Still, there was something so familiar in the silhouette that Del stood staring, disturbed.

Then the window was only a yellow, lamplit triangle and there were no shadows at all.

"I'm imagining things," he finally muttered. But the uneasiness persisted.

He could hear Rezin Bartee's hammer ringing on the anvil in the blacksmith shop. The glow of the newly ignited forge fire cast red spears of light from the door of the building as bellows fanned the coals.

Jefferson Street had cleared of ranch rigs, but there were still many saddle mounts along the street and the saloons and gambling houses were being patronized although it was still early for the real trade to begin.

He stood looking at the lighted fronts of the gambling places, tossing the silver dollar from hand to hand. In him was a surge of excitement. A presentiment, perhaps. A knowledge of a change in the tide of things. He had been aware of this mood only once before in his life, and that had been on the eve of the fight at Bloody Bend—a battle in which he should have been killed, but had emerged alive.

Two figures came from the door of Sun House across the street. One was Kathryn Camden. She was bareheaded, and had pulled a silk scarf around her neck. Her hair was very dark, very glossy in the bright glow of a battery of oil reflector lamps that lighted the entrance.

Her companion was a lean wiry man who wore the garb of an American cowboy. But he was a Mexican.

The lamplight reached Del across the street. He and the wiry, dark-complexioned man stared at each other for an instant.

Then, the wiry one, without a word, snatched a pistol from a holster hidden beneath his jacket. Del's hand swept instinctively to draw the six-shooter he had carried for so long in Mexico as one of Torreón's patriots. But it was not there. Torreón had not furnished him with weapons to defend himself when giving him his release.

He crouched, ducking aside, feeling that it was useless, for he was an easy target and he knew that this man across the street was no novice with a pistol.

He felt that he was as good as dead, and that might have been the case except for Kay Camden. With a cry, she threw herself against the wiry man an instant before he fired.

Del heard the bullet shatter glass in a window at his back, The bullet had missed him only by inches. The wiry man braced himself to fire again, swinging his sights to follow Del who was moving and zigzagging.

Kay Camden clung to his arm, screaming. He hurled her aside and she fell to the hotel steps.

The gun exploded again, but the man missed once more, unsteadied by her opposition and by Del's rush. But a third shot was coming. Del knew there was little chance of a miss at the narrowing range as he raced toward his opponent.

Powder flame flared down the street. Del heard the impact of a bullet on metal. The pistol was torn from the man's hand. He staggered back, blinded by fragments of metal. Del also felt the sting of particles. The bullet, fired from a distance, had struck the assassin's weapon, palpably by sheer luck.

The man tried to bring into play a derringer that he yanked from a hideout in his coat, but Del was on him like an avalanche. He knocked the derringer aside as it exploded, the shot going wide. His weight drove his quarry to the sidewalk and he rammed both knees savagely into the stomach, and smashed a fist to the face.

His victim lay gasping and contorted in agony. "You'll never get another chance like that," he panted. "I made the mistake of not packing a gun tonight, Marco."

He had never expected to encounter this man north of the border, for he had made a vow to kill him on sight. Now he had the chance. It would be so easy to throttle him. The urge was mighty, but suddenly it passed.

"No more killing," he said. "Not even you, Marco."

He looked up at Kay Camden. She was sitting on the hotel steps, her hair in disarray. She gazed at him speechlessly, her dark eyes big and frightened against her pallor.

"Don't you know you might have got shot!" Del said, his voice sharp. "Why take a chance like that?"

She just kept staring. He arose from the man he had felled and lifted her to her feet. He held her by the arms until she steadied.

"No damned Kittridge ever learned to say thanks for a favor," she gasped. "Did you expect me to just stand there and let him kill even you?"

Men came running. Thane Overmile, the town marshal, arrived. He peered at Del. "So I guessed right. It's you. In town half a day and in a gunscrape already."

He looked at the girl. "Are you hurt, Miss Camden?"

"No," she said.

The marshal bent, peering at the groaning man. "Who

58

is he?" he asked Del.

"I'd hardly say he's a friend of mine," Del said.

"Then what *do* you say? Do you want to name him?"

"Not in the presence of ladies," Del said.

Marshal Overmile smiled bleakly. "Well, I can tell you who be is. He's Marco Gonzales, one of Juan Torreón's *segundos*. Being as you were one of Torreón's men too, I'm quite sure you've met somewhere."

"Well, well!" Del said. "You're right. He is Marco Gonzales."

"Go and fetch Doc Abe, if he's to be found," the marshal said to a bystander.

"I doubt if he needs a doctor," Del said. "He's only got a numbed hand and the wind knocked out of him. Somebody shot his gun out of his hand."

"What happened, Miss Camden?" Overmile asked. "Did you see it?"

"All I know is that I came out of the hotel at the same time as this man. Mr. Kittridge was on the sidewalk across the street. This man drew his pistol. I saw that he intended to shoot Mr. Kittridge, who seemed to be unarmed, so I bumped into him before he fired. He pushed me away and again fired at Mr. Kittridge. As he tried to fire a third shot, a gun was fired down the street and the bullet struck his gun. Mr. Kittridge knocked him down then. He tried to shoot Mr. Kittridge with that little gun, but failed."

The marshal scanned the crowd that had gathered. "Who did the fancy shooting from down the street?" he asked.

Nobody answered. Overmile eyed Del. "Do you know?"

"No," Del said. "But I'd buy a drink for the one who

did it. I was running toward Gonzales and the shot came from my right."

Overmile shrugged. The marshal was a whipstock of a man, lithe and leathery and in his early forties, evidently. He had a reputation as a tough peace officer. Deadly with a pistol and efficient with his fists, he knew all the answers.

"Do you want me to jug you, Kittridge?" he asked.

"For what?"

"Your own protection, maybe. Gonzales might not have come across the line alone. I've been told that he double-crossed you down in Mexico and sold you out to Torreón's firing squad. That's why he started shootin' on sight, isn't it? He figured he had to beat you to the draw. He didn't know you didn't have a gun."

"I'll look after any more that show up," Del said.

"That means you'll be packing hardware from now on. This thing started out of my jurisdiction. Keep it there. I don't want your *insurrecto* quarrels settled here in Combabi. Keep them in Mexico. Or outside of town, at least."

Kay Camden started to move up the steps of the hotel. Del followed her and halted her. "Thanks," he said. "*Muchas gracias.*"

"I'd do the same for anyone," she said coldly. She added in a murmur that only he could hear. "My aunt is still waiting to speak to you. It's very important. And it's for your own good."

She turned her back on him and entered the lobby. He watched her vanish into the gilded cage of the elevator. She had failed to mention to the town marshal that she and her aunt had been talking with Marco Gonzales in their suite before the shooting and that she had not been on the sidewalk by chance. She had accompanied

60

Gonzales to the street, evidently to continue the conversation.

Marco Gonzales had been lifted to his feet by the marshal. He was keeping his lips clamped, evidently determined to say nothing. He did not look at Del.

"Keep in touch," Overmile said to Del. "You'll likely be called at the hearing."

"Hearing?"

"Gonzales crossed the line illegally, I'll hold him until the immigration boys from El Paso can take over. There'll be a hearing."

"I'm riding out to my place tonight," Del said. "You can find me there if I'm wanted."

"Your place?" Overmile asked wryly. "Rafter K. I was afraid it would be that when I first saw you in Combabi today."

"That's the way it is," Del said.

He pushed his way through the bystanders and walked down the street, heading for Tim Buttons' livery. Rezin Bartee was shedding his leather apron as Del passed the door of his shop. The forge fire was again banked. The tang of singed hoof hung in the air. A gray draft horse, hipshot to favor its new shoe, stood in the shop awaiting the return of its owner.

Rezin's eyes briefly met Del's. His left eyelid drooped a trifle.

"Thanks," Del murmured.

"Lucky shot," Rezin said. "I tried for a shoulder, but he was swinging around. The Lord was on his side."

Del walked onward. His father had told him that Rezin Bartee was the finest rifle shot he had ever seen. Luck had been with Marco Gonzales. Rezin had not been shooting to kill.

Reaching the livery, he found his horse in the stall he

61

had appropriated for it. But there was a padlock on the hasp.

"That'll be a dollar, six bits," Tim Buttons said. "Dollar fer boardin' the horse, the rest fer feed an' lookin' out fer your belongin's."

Buttons backed off a pace, a little frightened by his own greed. Del stood looking at him with distaste. There was no real anger in him. Only a sickness. Surely this must be the lowest of all low points in his life.

He recalled the moment he realized that he had been wrong about Juan Torreón and that the cause of liberation he had fought for was only another path to tyranny. That had been a time of disillusionment and self-accusation. A low point.

There had been the dawn not many days ago when he had been marched before one of Torreón's firing squads, only to be spared at the last minute. That had been an ending for him—but he had felt that it had also been a beginning. The start of a new life.

He still did not understand exactly why Torreón had permitted him to live in order to deliver to Walsh Camden's wife the message that her husband was being held hostage for the delivery of the horses Torreón needed. That message could have been sent by other means. Marco Gonzales could have brought it. And that led to the question as to why Gonzales had come to Combabi at all.

Now, Del had reached a new ebb—faced by a grasping stable owner who had the temerity to attempt to bilk him of a few pennies. The customary fee for the livery service Buttons had listed was less than half what he was asking.

"You figure I'll stand for your try at pocketpicking for fear Thane Overmile will take me to the calaboose if

I get mixed up in another ruckus, don't you, Tim?" he said.

Again he had the strange sensation of living over again an event of the past. Of following a pattern that had carried him along with it once before. Once more he was thinking of that day on Luzon when he should have been killed in battle, but had come through unscathed.

He thought of a half-naked Moro, leaping from the jungle at him, brandishing a bolo as he lay wounded and helpless. A shell from a Gatling gun had torn the life from the Moro before he could swing his weapon in the death stroke.

That same night, after the battle, his wound bandaged, he had won a thousand pesos in a game of Spanish monte, playing with other soldiers.

He palmed his silver dollar, tossed it in the air. "Tails I pull out," he said, "heads I try to run you into real money."

The dollar struck the dusty floor of the livery, bounced and came up heads.

Del pocketed it. "See that the padlock is off that stall when I come back," he said to Tim Buttons. He turned and left the livery, hearing Buttons gulp a sigh of thankfulness at his escape from reaping the fruits of his own rapacity.

CHAPTER 6

THERE WERE HALF A DOZEN GAMBLING PLACES TO choose from. Del headed for Jim Shanahan's Canary Cage. It was not the gaudiest establishment in Combabi, but he remembered it as the one where play was usually the highest. In addition, Jim Shanahan had a reputation for running honest games.

A yellow-haired soprano in an evening gown was singing a ballad to piano accompaniment on a tiny stage at the rear as Del entered. That ended and the curtain descended amid applause.

Play resumed at the tables. "The little ball rolls," a croupier at roulette droned. "Place your bets, gentlemen."

Dice rattled on tables. Case keepers and faro dealers returned to their stylized procedure.

Del walked to the bar and ordered a drink. That was stylized custom also. He called for a mug of beer and paid for it with one of his dimes. He sipped it while he sized up the action.

He knew many eyes were turning his way. A bouncer sat straighter in his lookout seat and glanced at the proprietor for orders. The answer from Jim Shanahan evidently was in the negative, for the man remained in his chair.

Shanahan was sitting at a rear table, playing poker with two men. That was where he had always played personally for the house, and the game had always been stud. It was stud now, Del saw. However, it was early in the evening, and the play seemed leisurely, the pots small.

Del finished his beer. The mirror on the back bar told him that his face had not suffered as much damage at Quinn Camden's hands as he had first believed. The court plaster covered a gash Quinn had inflicted on the cheekbone, and the swollen left eye was turning slightly in mourning. But the main damage had been to the body, and even those injuries evidently were only bruises of no lasting consequence.

He made his decision. As a rule he passed up roulette,

for he had never found pleasure in blind dependence on the chance that the white ball might favor his play. The same went for dice in his viewpoint.

He preferred poker where a man had some control over the outcome of the game. Luck, admittedly was a big factor, but along with it went skill, the ability to appraise an opponent's strength or weakness, to judge when to plunge or when to retreat.

Still, the odds at roulette were tremendous—if a man was lucky. He moved to the table where there were only two players who were desultorily scattering low-priced chips on the numbered squares.

He placed his dollar on the 1-12 combination and watched the ball spin, hop along the steel frets and come to rest.

"Number five comes up," the croupier intoned. He added two dollars to Del's fund.

Del placed one of the dollars on a number. Five. He lost.

He placed a second dollar on the same number. And won. The croupier pushed thirty-five stacked silver dollars his way.

Del placed ten dollars on the 1-12 combination and won again. He lost ten on the next roll, lost again.

He placed five dollars on the Double O. And hit.

The croupier looked at him. "Silver, gold, or chips?" he asked.

"Chips," Del said. He bet twenty dollars on a five-way combination and won again.

He asked for a sack and swept his chips into the canvas bag the croupier handed him. Jim Shanahan was still playing stud with the two men at the rear table.

Del knew both of Shanahan's opponents by sight and reputation. One was Otto Longabaugh, a cattle buyer who represented a big Chicago packing house in this part of New Mexico. He had been a commission agent for years, a profitable career. He was plump, well-dressed, and smoked a good cigar.

The other player was a lawyer, Leonard Willis. He too was well-dressed. He was graying at the temples, but it was a premature frosting, for Willis could be no more than forty. He was a tall, lithe man who apparently kept himself in good physical condition. Both he and Longabaugh had the looks of men able to take care of themselves in a stud game against even Jim Shanahan.

Del walked to the table. "Open game, gentlemen?" he asked.

"Yes," Shanahan said without hesitation and pointed to a vacant chair.

Del stacked his chips before him. They were in blues and whites. Ten-dollar and one-dollar denominations.

"I believe you and Otto are acquainted," Shanahan said. "Have you met Leonard Willis? Len, this is Del Kittridge, the son of an old friend of mine."

Del said, "Hello, Mr. Longabaugh. Nice knowing you, Mr. Willis." And shook hands.

Leonard Willis's grasp was strong, friendly. Longabaugh was neutral, noncommittal. Del had been surprised by the manner of Jim Shanahan's introduction. And warmed. He had not known that his father and the owner of the Canary Cage had been particularly friendly.

He looked at the gambler. "Thanks," he said.

Shanahan smiled. He understood. Del, as is the way of youth, had looked on men like Shanahan as well up in years. Now, it came to him that Shanahan, like Leonard Willis, was far from that. Shanahan looked the part of what he was—the tough, hoarse-voiced owner of a high play gambling house in a rough town, but he too could scarcely be more than forty, and was palpably able to take care of himself in case of trouble.

All the action Shanahan had seen had not been at gambling tables. He had a reputation as a fast man with a six-shooter and at rough-and-tumble barroom fighting. He dressed quietly in a dark sack suit, soft white shirt and a dark, four-in-hand tie. No doubt there was on him somewhere a six-shooter, but not even a bulge in the tailored coat betrayed its whereabouts.

There was a stern pride in Jim Shanahan. Pride in himself and his record for honesty. The house percentage was his margin of profit. His own skill at cards was his real edge. He could and had been beaten, both in skill and by runs of luck on the parts of opponents. He had been on the verge of being cleaned out a time or two. But he had never closed his table as long as a patron wanted action. He had never placed a limit on the betting.

But he was a professional gambler. Once a man bought cards in Jim Shanahan's game, let him beware. Gambling, with Shanahan, was cold-blooded, merciless.

"Luck follows a winner," Shanahan had often said. "And to win, you can't be soft. Ride your luck when you have it. Ride it hard."

He had and would take the last dollar from any one who sat in his game. Or loan his own last cent to a friend in need. His skill was so uncanny at stud that only experts had a chance with him.

The play was easy at first. Casual. Almost dull. For a time it went that way. Friendly. Relaxed. Nobody won or lost much.

Del was enjoying the play. He believed he was slightly ahead. But he didn't count his chips. He was not superstitious in most things but he believed, beyond question, there was such a thing as luck, good and bad, at cards.

He was following Shanahan's creed, riding the tide. He felt that his luck had come in there in the street when Kay Camden had been at Marco, Gonzales' side so that she could upset his aim. Also when Rezin Bartee had been in a position to use his rifle.

Even now, during this period of quiet play, he had the warm, solid feeling that fortune was still with him. The proper term probably was confidence. He had started with a dollar. Even when he had placed it on the roulette table there had been the assurance in his mind that he would win.

He still held that heady sensation. Each time he pushed chips in the pot to buy a card, he bet with confidence. He was not running scared. Nor was he betting with scared money.

He pushed his luck. He had learned from experience that it was jealous. It was fickle. Once scorned, or finding its smile being wasted on weakness, it would leave as mysteriously as it had come.

Luck, confidence, belief in himself, assurance. Whatever it was, he rode the tide and began forcing the play, bluffing when he sensed an uncertainty in the opposition, piling in the chips when he held an advantage.

The game warmed. He had been sitting there more than an hour and saw that his chips had tripled. They were all blues now. Smaller denominations had been cashed in and removed from the table as a nuisance.

Shanahan was the heaviest loser. Otto Longabaugh was well down also. Leonard Willis was slightly ahead. Willis was cool and without emotion in his play, but in him Del sensed there was the killer instinct of the true gambler. Willis was like a hawk, soaring motionless in the sky, his eyes on the prey, waiting the moment to strike.

Looking up, Del discovered that the Canary Cage had become crowded. The bar was lined two-deep with men. Other games were in full operation but the play at Shanahan's table was the center of attraction.

The deal passed to Len Willis. "Seven-card stud for this round," he said.

They had been playing almost exclusively the formal five-card game. Seven-card stud meant three cards down and four up. It was a rough game, dangerous, unpredictable.

Shanahan shrugged wryly. He preferred the orthodox game, but offered no protest.

Del's first down card was the spade ace. His second down card was a king of hearts. His first up card was a trey.

Len Willis was high on the table with a queen. He bet ten dollars and everyone stayed.

Del caught a king as his next up card, giving him a pair. Shanahan had a pair of jacks showing, Longabaugh a pair of tens. Leonard Willis had only a queen and a nine in sight.

Shanahan, high on the table, bet fifty dollars. Longabaugh met the bet. Willis studied his cards for a moment. "Tilt it a hundred," he said.

A stir ran around the room, and the play at other tables slowed as attention swung. Everyone in the Canary Cage seemed to sense it at the same time. The big hand was coming up. In high play games it always came up sooner or later.

Del, with his king and ace in the hole and the king

and trey showing, pushed in chips. "Staying," he said. The price was one hundred and fifty dollars.

Longabaugh scowled, grunted, and finally met the raise. Shanahan also called.

Del received an ace as his third up card. He now had pairs, kings, and aces. But concealed. Shanahan and Longabaugh failed to improve their strength in sight, catching a deuce and a nine, respectively.

Shanahan's jacks were still high on the board. He checked the bet to Willis, trying for a test of strength.

Willis had a queen, nine, and ten showing. A possible straight. Not a strong hand in a seven-card game.

Willis counted out twenty chips. "Two hundred," he said.

Del met the bet, staying. So did Longabaugh, again with reluctance. Shanahan tilted it by fifty dollars, again obviously trying to smoke out Willis's determination.

It was Willis's turn to meet the raise. Again, coolly, he counted out stacks of chips. "And three hundred more," he said. "Thirty-five blues, if I'm correct."

The strength had been exposed. Or had it? Willis's hand showed nothing on the board except the possible weak straight. He either had power in his down cards, or was running a bluff.

Del decided Willis was bluffing. "And two hundred more," he said, pushing in the chips.

Longabaugh groaned and tossed in his cards, dropping out of the pot. "Man overboard," he lamented.

Shanahan chewed a dead cigar and met the two raises. "I didn't aim to kick over a hornet's nest," he complained mildly.

Del watched Leonard Willis. This was the critical moment. If the man was bluffing, he might try to clinch it by another heavy raise. Or he might decide he was wasting money and would drop out. For there was little doubt that Shanahan was either banking on picking up a full house, or might have one already, even though he had only the pair of jacks showing.

Willis pushed in chips. "I'll see Mr. Kittridge and also another card," he said.

The chips on the table represented around three thousand dollars. Rigid silence had settled over the room.

Willis flipped out the fourth up cards. Del caught a trey. He now held three pairs. Kings, aces, treys. The graveyard hand. The sort of hand that had lured many players to ruin. Weak at the moment, yet possessing the maddening probability of filling into a full house. And a powerfull at that with aces and kings waiting, and none of these cards having appeared an the board in opponents' hands.

Willis and Shanahan did not improve their hands in sight.

Strength in all hands was concealed. Del was certain of one thing. He believed he had proved that Leonard Willis was not bluffing and that he was seeking, or already had more strength than a medium straight.

Shanahan palpably must have a full house, and its top, no doubt, was three jacks.

Shanahan, cautious now, again checked the, bet to Willis.

"Five hundred," Willis said.

Everyone sighed and watched Del. He debated it for a time. He now decided that Willis also had a full house. Queens on top, probably. By the rule of thumb his chances were as good as theirs of filling, in case they were gambling on that possibility. Even better than their chances, perhaps, because of his three pairs.

71

He had lost the three pots previous to this big one—the longest losing streak of the night for him. Had the tide changed? Had fickle fortune deserted him?

He pushed in the five hundred. Shanahan made a wry gesture and tossed in his cards. "Never throw good money after bad," he said.

Willis dealt the last cards, face down, to Del and himself. Del tilted a corner of the card. An ace. His luck had held. He had filled an ace full on kings. Powerful.

Willis studied Del's shrunken stack of chips. "I'll tap you for it, Kittridge," he said.

"This isn't a table stakes game, Mr. Willis," Del said. "You're entitled to hit me as hard as you decide."

Willis shrugged. "So be it," he said.

He pushed in ten stacks of chips. "A thousand," he said.

Del counted his chips. He had exactly twenty-one blues. Two hundred and ten dollars' worth. He sat considering it. He could toss in his cards, and still quit the game more than two hundred dollars ahead of his original stake.

He did not consider offering an IOU or a promissory note. He took it for granted that the Kittridge credit rating was far from gilt-edge in Combabi. Nor could he ask Jim Shanahan for a loan. Shanahan had a rigid rule against backing players in gambling at his tables.

Del looked around. He saw that Quinn and Cullen Camden were among the onlookers. They stood at the crowded bar, glasses in their hands. Quinn had a swollen jaw. He was trying to grin mockingly at Del's predicament, but the effort turned out to be painfully lopsided. Cullen Camden evidently had been drinking heavily, but his expression was difficult to interpret.

Rezin Bartee was also in the Canary Cage, standing

nearby.

"Could you give me a little time?" Del asked Len Willis.

Willis nodded. "Certainly."

Del placed his cards in line on the table. "It might take a little while," he said. "Please be patient."

He arose to leave and Jim Shanahan beckoned to Rezin. "Sit in for Mr. Kittridge until he returns, Rezin," he said. "Meanwhile we'll all have a sociable drink. What will be the pleasure of you gentlemen?"

Del strode out of the Canary Cage. The only place he felt he had a chance of raising money would be the bank. That institution would be closed at this hour, of course, especially on a national holiday, but Del hoped he could find Ed Donally and arrange a loan.

He headed for Sun House, hoping he might find Donally there, or at least be able to learn his whereabouts. However, passing the bank, he saw bright lamplight back of the frosted glass in the president's private office.

He mounted the stone steps and rapped on the gilt-lettered glass of the front door. The door of the inner office opened and Ed Donally emerged. He still had on his frock coat and wilted collar. He also had picked up a silver-mounted, double-barreled buckshot gun before stepping into the open foyer, and he had it half-cocked and ready.

He peered through the glass and recognized Del. The gun lifted a trifle higher. "What'n tophet do *you* want?" he called.

"A loan," Del replied. "Eight hundred dollars. Open up, and I'll explain."

"I'm busy and you must be drunk," Donally raged. "If you really want money come tomorrow at regular—"

73

He paused. Del had the impression that someone else had spoken. Evidently someone was in the inner office.

Donally, scowling, unbarred the door. He kept the shotgun ready to fire as Del stepped in. "What do you want money for at this hour of the night?" he demanded.

"I'm in a poker game at the Canary Cage," Del said. "There's five thousand or close to it in the pot and I've got a hand I think will take it. But I'm eight hundred dollars short of calling the other man."

"Who's the other man?" Donally asked caustically. "Jim Shanahan, I suppose."

"No. Leonard Willis, the lawyer."

Donally uttered a snort. "That's just as bad. Len's a smart poker player. This is a bank, not a gambling house. Do you think a bank would lend money on a poker hand?"

"I've got title to a section of land on Castle Creek," Del said. "I'll put it up as security on a ninety-day note at interest. That's banking business, isn't it? It won't be a gamble—for the bank at least."

Donally's attitude changed. "I see. It's a mite unusual, of course, but maybe we just can get together on—"

A new voice spoke. "I might back your poker hand, Mr. Kittridge."

The bank's visitor had arisen from a chair in the inner office and stepped in sight in the open door. Harriet Camden. The Lady of Two Star.

She added, "Provided, of course, that I consider it a sound gamble."

"Harriet!" Ed Donally exploded.

"Don't Harriet me!" she said. "You know you're aching to buy into that hand, Ed. And not with the bank's money. With your own. You know it's a good

74

risk."

She turned to Del and inspected him frowningly. "You've been fighting, haven't you? I don't imagine you find yourself too welcome in Combabi. Who was the other man?"

Del ignored the question. "I prefer to deal with the bank. Or with Donally."

"I'll offer better terms than either of them. Ed will charge you a stiff rate of interest. I'll do much better."

"Such as?"

"A third of the pot."

Del cocked an eyebrow. "A third? That would add up to about seventeen hundred dollars. Is that what you call better terms?"

"But, if you lose, you will owe me nothing," she said. "With Ed, you'd be in debt for what you borrowed. With interest."

A second visitor had been in the inner office. Kay Camden. She appeared and joined her aunt. She quietly watched Del, awaiting his answer.

"I'm risking eight hundred dollars," Harriet Camden said. "You're risking your land if you borrow from the bank."

"Do you mean you're not asking my land as security?"

"No. This is a poker game. A gambling proposition."

"What if Willis tops me after I call?"

"Then we both lose. What else?"

"Harriet!" Ed Donally began. "Walsh won't like this. He would—"

She ignored him. "But, as I said, Mr. Kittridge, I'll back you only if I consider it a sound bet. What kind of a hand do you hold? What's the strength of Len's hand?"

75

Del studied her, trying to, decide exactly what motive she might have. There had always been talk that Harriet Camden had a wild streak. It was common knowledge that she could ride to hounds as recklessly as any man in the hunting parties that her husband had once organized at Two Star, She could handle a bird gun over field dogs so expertly she was often called on by Eastern sporting friends to take charge of their entries in competitive shows.

Her ability as a horsewoman was so commonplace it attracted comment only from strangers. Stories of how she played poker at Two Star with men often scandalized the housewives of the Combabi country. She was said to have a taste for champagne and even smoked cigarettes in public if the mood suited her.

"Aces full o n kings," Del said, suddenly making his decision. "Willis has a queen, nine, four, and deuce showing. It's seven-card stud."

"Seven-card," she said. "A hard game to analyze. Go over the deal card by card. And the betting."

Del did so, describing each round and the wagering.

Harriet Camden listened intently without interrupting, then sat thinking, her lips pursed. "What's your belief?" she finally asked.

"A queen full at best, on either nines, fours, or deuces," Del said. "He's got more than a plain straight. That's for sure."

Kay Camden spoke. "He *could* have four queens."

"Yes," Del said.

"That would mean he'd have three queens down," Harriet Camden said. "The odds against that are tremendous."

"Anything's possible in poker," Del said.

"How much of your own money do you have at stake

76

in this pot, Mr. Kittridge?" Kay Camden asked caustically.

"A dollar," Del said.

"A dollar!" She and her aunt looked at each other, wide-eyed. They burst into laughter that was almost hysterical.

"Very well," Harriet Camden said. "I believe you're justified in calling Len. He's one to try to run you out of a game with a worthless hand. He might have nothing at all. It would be just like him, the scamp."

"It's going to cost Two Star eight hundred dollars to find out, Harriet," Ed Donally protested. "Walsh can't afford—"

She silenced him with a look. "Please get the money, Ed. This will be from my own personal fund, not Star's."

She eyed Del. "Is this agreeable? Do you accept my offer of throwing in with you for one-third interest. I assure you, it's the best offer you will get."

"I don't seem to have a choice," Del said. "Apparently, the bank has washed its hands of this. You understand, of course, that you can lose?"

"I understand," she sighed. "Oh, how I understand about losing money."

"And cattle," her niece said.

"Please, Kathryn!" Harriet Camden remonstrated.

Kay Camden said nothing more, but she was hostile, unforgiving.

Donally reluctantly retreated into an inner room of the bank. He returned presently with a pack of bills and handed it to Harriet Camden. She coolly counted the money, signed a receipt, and handed it over to Del.

"Do I sign something also?" Del asked.

"That won't be necessary," Harriet Camden said.

77

"You mean you'd trust a Kittridge with this cash with nothing to show for it?"

He was addressing Kay Camden rather than her aunt. She did not respond, but her gaze remained scornful.

Harriet Camden arose. "Please come to the hotel afterward, Mr. Kittridge. Kay and I are going to our rooms. We will wait there."

"What if I lose?"

"Come anyway. There's something I want to discuss with you. Something very important."

There it was again. The arrogance. The Camden command.

"I'll let you know how I come out," Del said shortly.

He walked out of the bank, carrying the bills in his hand.

He entered the Canary Cage. Men who had been relaxing, came to attention with a shuffle of boots.

He walked to the poker table and said, "Never mind getting up, Rezin. This won't take long."

He counted the bills and placed the packet on top of the chips on the table. "I'm calling, Mr. Willis," he said.

Leonard Willis turned over, one by one, his three hole cards. A queen. A queen. A queen. With the queen showing he held four of a kind.

Del gazed at the cards. "The odds," he said, "were tremendous, as a person just told me. You're too strong for my full house."

He tossed his hand into the discards along with those of Shanahan and Otto Longabaugh. "Good night, gentlemen," he said. "I enjoyed playing with you."

He picked up the one blue chip that remained of his stack. "I'll. buy you a drink, Rezin," he said. "I need one."

He and Rezin drank at the bar amid silence. Del

78

picked up the change the barkeeper gave him for the chip he had placed down in payment, pocketed it and walked out into the street. The cooling night wind helped a little.

CHAPTER 7

ONCE AGAIN HE MOVED TOWARD TIM BUTTONS' livery. Rezin laid a hand on his arm. "Where are you goin'?"

"Out to the place," Del said. "To Rafter K."

"There's nothin' there, Del. No house. Nothin' but the graves. Lottie's and John's."

"I'm used to sleeping on the ground. I've got my bedroll."

He added, "You can do one thing for me, Rezin, if you will. Go to Sun House and tell Lady Camden that we were both wrong. It *is* possible to have three queens in the hole."

He left Rezin standing there and walked to the livery. Tim Buttons was still on duty. He came out of the office where he had been playing checkers with a cowboy and watched as Del retrieved his belongings and saddled the steeldust.

Del handed him a dollar. "That's still more than the usual price," he said. "That's all even a Kittridge will pay."

Buttons stood silently by while he mounted and rode out of the stable. Looking back as he rode down Jefferson Street, he saw Rezin entering Sun House, palpably puzzled and disturbed by the errand Del had given him.

Del wondered how Harriet Camden would take the

loss. Eight hundred dollars would not have amounted to much in the Camden scheme of things in the past. But now . . .

As he rode westward away from Combabi, he continued to puzzle over why she had financed him. He could not find a solid answer.

After an hour, Castle Dome's rounded top began to take shape against the stars. Before midnight, his horse waded the Castle Creek ford and he was on his own land. After the hard years. After Cuba. After the Philippines. After following a false cause in Mexico. Fighting years. They now seemed to have been wasted years. For he had seen the waste of war.

He picketed the steeldust on graze, carried his bedroll to the stream and spread his tarp beneath a big black willow in whose shade he had swum on hot summer days with his father in a pool they had formed by damming the stream with logs and rocks. The dam was still intact.

He was practically penniless. In his camp pack were a few scraps of food, jerky and corn meal that Torreón had given him to carry him out of Mexico. There was scarcely enough to sustain him more than a day. Still, he slept soundly and contentedly. He was home.

He awakened with the rising sun in his eyes. He lay for a time, listening to sounds that had been familiar to him during the golden years of boyhood. Wrens and jays scolded in the brush and squirrels grumbled an answer. A crow cawed. He identified the soft thudding sound as made by the feet of a jackrabbit that had come down to the stream to drink.

Half asleep, half awake, he waited for signs of other activity—of the stir of the saddlestring in the corral as the horses awaited the morning ration of hay; the cook rattling ashes from the stove as be hurried breakfast for the riders. He listened for his mother's wonderful voice, talking to his father in the kitchen.

But all he heard were the crow and the small sounds of the wrens and the jackrabbit. An emptiness and almost a terror came. He had been listening for ghosts, for sounds from the dead. His contentment was shattered. He lay, desolate and confused. Again came the doubt—the doubt that he should ever have come back to the Combabi. Already, the old hostilities were flaring.

He finally arose. He swam in the pool and that cleared his thoughts. His doubts faded. But not the loneliness. He built a small fire and breakfasted on salt meat and corn meal cakes. He set the coffee to boil in a tin and walked out of the brush into the open flat.

His father had built the house on a rise that commanded a view southward as far as the Purple Mountains that straddled the border. This was the heart of the Combabi, which was really a basin, surrounded by broken mountain uplifts. It was rich cattle range. Rare in the border country, it had running creeks, even in the arid summers, fed by the surrounding mountains.

The ranchhouse that Dave Kittridge had built of rock blasted from nearby Castle Dome and from cedar logs that he had felled and adzed into shape in the Emeralds, was no longer there. Nor the bunkhouse or cook's shack. Nothing. Even the barn and corrals were gone. Del walked across the flat, a rage rising in him again, a rage that had been just below the surface all these years.

Not a stick, not a stone could he find of anything that his father had built. It was as Rezin Bartee had said. Walsh Camden had not only leveled Rafter K and burned the timbers, but he had plowed the ashes under

81

and had buried even the foundation stones. Brush, bunch grass, and tumbleweeds had invaded the disturbed earth.

The fury mounted as he stood gazing, trying to orient himself—and failing. Walsh Camden had done so thorough a job of obliteration that it was difficult to determine exactly where the house had stood. And had the cook's shack been just about here? Or to the right a rod or so. There was no sure way of telling.

Along with the anger was almost an awe at the violence of Walsh Camden's wrath. What was it that had turned two men from friends into such bitter enemies? The easy answer was greed. The obvious explanation seemed to be Walsh Camden's thirst to own more and more range.

But that hardly explained the savagery with which the Two Star owner had tried to erase every evidence of Dave Kittridge's very existence in the Combabi. Walsh Camden had not only destroyed his former friend physically and financially, but had tried to wipe out every trace that Dave Kittridge had ever lived.

Del's attention swung to a green plot of grass in the shade of wild pecans and post oaks near the creek. It had been a picnic spot when his parents had entertained guests on hot summer days. He could hear his coffee boiling over, the liquid sizzling in the embers. Ignoring it, he strode toward the grove which stood on a rise above reach of overflows from the creek.

The oblong of green grass was watered by means of a line of tile pipe brought from the creek somewhere upstream. The grass was being trimmed regularly and there was a small tool shack nearby in which he saw garden implements. A strong wire fence had been built to bar cattle and deer from the plot and the two graves that lay there.

Del lifted the latch on the gate to the plot and entered. He stood looking at the two mounds. There were head markers, made of wood, with the names and dates of the deaths of his father and mother carved in the surface, and newly repainted in black:

LOTTIE DELANEY KITTRIDGE
beloved wife of David Welton Kittridge
1859-1896

DAVID WELTON KITTRIDGE
beloved husband and father
1857-1898

MURDERED!

Murdered! Del bent closer, peering. He had made those grave markers himself, hewed them from mountain cedar that he had felled in the Emeralds. He had carved the names of his parents and added the dates of their births and deaths on the wood.

But someone had added the word "Murdered!" It had been deeply burned in the wood with a hot iron.

He became aware he was not alone with his dead. He turned. Harriet Camden and her niece sat on saddlehorses at a distance, watching him. They evidently had arrived by way of the ford and had pulled up, waiting until he became aware of their presence.

He left the little cemetery, latching the gate, and walked toward them.

"I take it that we have permission to dismount," Harriet Camden said.

Without waiting for an answer, she alighted. Her

niece, however, remained mounted in the custom of the country.

Del smiled grimly. "It can't be that at least one of the Camdens is turning humble and knows proper manners. Permission granted, Kathryn."

He moved, intending to offer a hand, but Kay Camden swung swiftly from the saddle, pointedly refusing his assistance.

Her aunt spoke. "It was unfortunate that you failed to comply with my request for a talk last evening. Rezin Bartee brought word of the sad outcome of my poker venture."

"Sad for both of us," Del said. "We both could have used the money."

She ignored that. "Since the mountain did not come to me, I have come to the mountain. I want you to help me get my husband out of Juan Torreón's hands."

It took Del by complete surprise. "I must have misunderstood you, ma'am. Are you sure you know who you're talking to? I'm Dave Kittridge's son. Remember?"

"I remember. Only too well. That's why I want you to take charge of delivering the horses to Torreón."

"I still can't be hearing right," Del said. "Are you really asking me to try to run three hundred head of stock into Mexico just to save Walsh Camden's hide?"

"Exactly."

"Any particular reason why I would do a thing like that?"

"From my viewpoint, it would probably save my husband's life. From your viewpoint it will be for profit. I believe your cash resources are, shall we say, limited?"

"And just what would be my profit?" Del asked.

84

"Half of the price of the horses."

Del laughed. "Half of nothing. You really don't dream that Juan Torreón will pay anything for those horses if he ever got his hands on them?"

"Even so you will get your money. I don't value my husband's life in terms of cash. Torreón offered a hundred dollars a head. Half of that will bring you fifteen thousand dollars. I'll see that you are paid, regardless of whether Torreón pays us."

Del eyed her. She had just lost eight hundred dollars in backing his poker hand. From Ed Donally's attitude, that had strained her own private sources. She was now offering a gamble for fifteen thousand dollars.

She guessed his thoughts. "It happened that I inherited some money in my own right from my family," she said. "I also own title to Two Star headquarters and two sections of the creek frontage on which it stands. I will mortgage that, if necessary. I made the arrangements with Ed Donally last night. You will get your fifteen thousand dollars."

"Why did you back that poker hand?" Del asked abruptly.

She answered disdainfully. "As you have pointed out, I could have used the money. I'm sure that Rezin Bartee has brought you up to date on our situation at Two Star. We are not as prosperous as in better days, thanks to your father."

"And the other reasons?"

She was coldly frank. "I wanted to place you under obligation to me. I expected it would bring you to Sun House last night where we could discuss the matter that brought me here."

Del looked around at his small empire. A few thousand dollars might put Rafter K well on the road back, give him the foundation on which to rebuild what had been destroyed.

"No," he said. "That's my answer."

Kay Camden spoke. "Surely, you're not refusing on ethical grounds? Not you—a Kittridge?"

Del looked at her. "If you mean I'd refuse to do anything that might help a leppie like Juan Torreón, the answer is yes. But, in this case, selling him horses would be more likely to destroy him than help him. It wouldn't be a crime, the way I look at it."

"A strange way of looking at it. I'd consider three hundred horses quite a lot of help to a precious rascal like that."

"You're not quite as well acquainted with affairs in Mexico as I am. This horse deal might be only giving Torreón more rope with which to hang himself. He's not the only liberator who's turned out to be a cutthroat down there. There are others. Like Tony Carrosco. Carrosco above all. He and Torreón are bitter enemies. Give each of them enough guns, enough horses, enough bullets, and they'll destroy each other."

"A cynical attitude," Kay Camden said.

"A practical one in dealing with men like that. They are the most cynical humans I've ever known."

"Cynical or not, I must admit you have eased my conscience," Harriet Camden said. "The matter of dealing with Juan Torreón involved questions of right and wrong that I tried not to ask myself. I trust that you are right. I may have enough to answer for without having to atone for helping a man like that."

She added, "Now that the matter of ethics has been taken care of, there's no earthly reason why you can't do what needs to be done."

"Why me?"

"Because I want to be sure the horses have a good chance of reaching their destination."

"I'm positive that isn't aimed at being a compliment," Del said.

"Hardly. It's a statement of fact."

"What you mean is that you need an experienced border hopper. A man who knows how to run stock into Mexico under the noses of the law."

"Exactly."

"In other words, a Long Rider."

"Long Riders," she corrected him. "You can't do this alone, of course. I'm sure you can get in touch with men who are equally experienced in running the border."

"Are you proposing that the Kittridge Long Riders come back from the tomb and start running stock across the line again?"

"If you want to put it that way—yes."

He glanced toward the plot of green on the knoll. "I'm afraid they won't all be able to come back from the tomb."

He believed he saw a twinge of pain on her lips. She did not let her eyes turn in that direction. "You will do this," she said. "You must."

"You've heard of Pandora's box," he said.

"Yes."

"These were desperate men. They might not be shoved back into the box if they're brought back to life again."

"I'm fully aware of that risk. Only too well. It was Two Star they hated. It was only Two Star they preyed on. I remember the Big Raid. That was even after their leader was dead. Your father. Two Star has never recovered from that."

"You must also know that it's too much to ask of

them," he said. "This isn't a matter of running cattle across the line. This is like war. The United States is out to do all it can to put an end to men like Torreón without actually going to war with Mexico. Horses are contraband, along with anything else that will help these raiders. It was only the Rangers that border hoppers had to deal with in the past. Now, it's the United States Army. Anyone caught running horses will wind up in Leavenworth."

She remained stonily unmoved. "I am aware of all this. Also that Torreón sentenced you to a firing squad and probably will have you shot if you fall into his hands again. I'm sure, however, that you took risks almost as great as a border jumper with your father and for far less reward than I'm offering. Fifteen thousand dollars is a tidy sum."

"You really don't expect me to turn a finger to help Walsh Camden? Not for money? Not for anything on earth?"

"He's my husband. If it's more money you want, I'll do my best. I can scrape up perhaps another five thou—"

"You've come to the wrong place. And to the wrong man."

He turned and started to walk away. A gun exploded. The bullet ripped a furrow from the earth almost beneath the sole of his boot. The slug cut the ground from beneath his step. He staggered, straightened.

Harriet Camden stood with a .38 in her hand, powder fumes drifting. Her eyes were gray and hard as granite.

Del took another stride. Again a slug cut the ground from beneath his step. He tried another step. Another bullet. It was fancy shooting. He had escaped having a foot maimed only by the amazing accuracy of the

88

woman who stood calmly sure of herself as she balanced the pistol, ready to fire again.

"Better notch a little higher," he said. "You're missing me."

"I'm not through talking to you," she said.

"Wrong," Del said. "We're finished."

"You're the one who's wrong. I have a message for you, from—"

"No!" Kay Camden almost screamed. "No, Aunt Harriet! You promised—"

She had grasped her aunt's arm in an attempt to silence her. Harriet Camden thrust her away. "This message came from Juan Torreón, Mr. Kittridge," she said. "It was for you."

Del stiffened. "Go on!" he said harshly.

"Do you know a Mexican woman named Amata Villareal?"

A clammy hand seemed to touch him. "Yes," he said.

"And one named Carlota?"

"Carlota is Amata Villareal's daughter. About six years old."

Harriet Camden suddenly seemed less sure of herself. "Your wife?" she asked. "Your daughter?"

"No," Del said.

"But you know them?"

"Amata is the widow of a very close friend. Carlos Villareal. He was tortured by Juan Torreón and shot by a firing squad before my eyes. That was not many days ago. It was the morning Torreón turned me loose so that I could bring word to you about your husband."

"I see. A very close friend, you say. Then—"

"Stop this!" her niece burst out. "It isn't fair!"

"What isn't fair?" Del demanded. "What about Amata Villareal?"

Harriet Camden's expression was stony. "The message from Torreón told me to inform you that he knew where to find this woman and her child."

She backed away a pace, appalled in spite of herself, by Del's expression.

"You're lying!" he said. "You must be lying. How—?"

Then he guessed the answer. "Marco Gonzales! So that's why he followed me to Combabi. Torreón sent him."

"Yes," Harriet Camden said. Her voice was shaky. "He came to see me at Sun House yesterday afternoon after the parade."

Del looked at Kay Camden. "So that's why you we're so sure. You knew this when you came to that carnival tent."

She was ashen. "Yes," she said reluctantly.

"Sure of what?" her aunt demanded.

"Sure that you had the whiphand over me," Del said. "Sure that I'd have to throw in with you against Torreón."

Harriet Camden did not answer. But there was triumph in her eyes. Her niece turned away. She was hiding sudden tears.

"But Gonzales talked to you at Sun House after dark, not in the afternoon," Del said. "I saw him there just before he tried to kill me."

"He came back to find out if I had made the arrangements to have you run the horses. He was very angry because I had not. He was insistent that I go to you at once and tell you about the Señora Villareal. He seemed to be sure it would influence you."

"He was right. Do you know exactly what you're asking?"

90

"I'm asking only that my husband will return safe and unharmed."

"I soldiered with Carlos Villareal. I got to know him better than any person I'd ever met. He wasn't meant to be a soldier. He was a dreamer, a thinker. A poet. He could paint. He painted things that looked crazy, but kept drawing you deeper and deeper into, their color and beauty."

"I'm sure I am not interested in your friend," Harriet Camden said. But there was a desperation in her—and a terror.

"Carlos was a visionary," Del said. "He despised pomp and conceit. And little tyrants. We both joined Juan Torreón when he first took the field. He was for liberty and justice too—at first."

He paused, gazing southward toward the Purples. Toward Mexico whose mystery lay beyond those mountain rims. "How wrong we were. He changed. We did not. Power went to his head. He turned out to be only another mercenary, out to exploit the people he had betrayed."

He looked at Harriet Camden. "Carlos and Amata were in love. Deeply in love. Can you really understand something like that? She's the daughter of a Mexican patriot who was wealthy. A decent, upstanding man who also opposed Torreón. She is a beautiful woman. Educated, refined. Carlota will be a beautiful woman also when she grows up."

He added, "*If* she grows up. Carlos threw in with me when I turned against Torreón. We began raising an army to fight him. Marco Gonzales pretended to be one of us. He sold us into Torreón's hands. He was even the officer in charge of the firing squad that executed Carlos and was to shoot me."

91

"Gonzales?" Kay Camden exclaimed. "Then that's why—!"

Del nodded. "Why he tried to kill me last night. He knew I would shoot him on sight. He took it for granted I was armed. I see now why they let me go, so as to bring word they had Walsh Camden. They need horses even more than Torreón wants to have me shot. But they weren't really turning me loose. They knew they had a string on me that would bring me back into Mexico."

Neither Harriet nor her niece spoke.

"When Gonzales turned traitor, we managed to get word to Amata in time, and she escaped into hiding with Carlota," Del said. "Torreón would have used them as a club to force Carlos and myself to tell him the details of our organization. Principally to give him the names of other men who were in it with us."

He paused for a moment, then added, "But now he's found them."

"He wouldn't—?" Kay began, her voice thin.

"I'm afraid he would," Del said.

He gazed again at the land that had been his home and that he had hoped would be the birthplace of a new Rafter K. He looked once more toward the Purples in Mexico.

He was no longer a free man. Or even a man alive. He had not escaped Juan Torreón's firing squad. It had only been a reprieve.

"Torreón could have been lying," Kay Camden said desperately. "It could only be a trick. He might not really know where Amata Villareal is hiding."

Del nodded. "Yes. He could be lying."

She hesitated. "Then, you won't—"

She broke off. Del was looking at Harriet Camden. "You know I will, don't you, ma'am?" he said harshly.

"You know you hold high card this time. I've got to make sure. I know where Amata is—or should be, I've got to know if she's safe, or if I can help her, if Torreón has really got her."

He added, "I'll try to run the horses. How soon can you round up three hundred head?"

Harriet Camden gazed at him, and for a moment he had the impression that within her was a searing sense of shame and guilt. Then she straightened. Once more she was the imperious mistress of Two Star. "As soon as—"

Her niece interrupted her. "The offer is withdrawn." She looked at her aunt. "Don't you understand, Aunt Harriet? You're as much as asking Mr. Kittridge to go to his death. We must find someone else to help us."

"You're a little late," Del said grimly. "I've got to go back into Mexico. And not for Walsh Camden's sake. At least I'll have a powerful hole card too. Better than the ones I held at the Canary Cage last night. Thirty thousand dollars' worth of horseflesh will be a mighty strong hand to sit in with. Torreón needs those horses above everything else in the world. Above my life, above Amata's life, and least of all, Walsh Camden's."

"Come to the ranch this afternoon and we will work out a plan," Harriet Camden said.

"I'll ride with you now, at once," Del said. "Hours count. Torreón is an impatient man. I'll rig my horse."

He added, "There's one condition. If I or any of the Long Riders go into Mexico to help Walsh Camden, then there must be Camdens along. If blood is to be spilled, or prison for some of us, let Camdens take their chances too."

Harriet Camden flushed. "You know better than to imply that my sons would fail in their duty to their father. Quinn and Cullen will ride with you." But Del

93

saw that within her was a doubt—and shame and uncertainty. He saw these same emotions in her niece.

Harriet Camden turned and mounted her horse. "Do you know you are the living image of your father when he was your age?" she said abruptly.

It was so unexpected, he had no answer. Her sadness drove a weird uneasiness through him. He had the sensation of having touched on something dark and elusive and dreadful.

He turned to offer help to Kay Camden, but she was already swinging into the saddle. Her aunt rode side-saddle, but she was astride, wearing a divided habit.

While the two visitors waited, he doused the embers of his breakfast fire, scoured his utensils with water and sand and hung his meager belongings from a limb out of reach of packrats and porcupines.

He again gazed at the flat where the house had once stood, knowing that the chances were that he might never see this place again.

Turning to mount, he found Kay Camden watching him. Her hostility had melted, for the moment at least. In her was a brooding regret—troubled thoughts.

She turned away, but he felt that she had understood the bleak frustration in him—and sympathized.

He mounted and joined them. The sun was hot in the morning sky as they headed down the range toward Two Star.

CHAPTER 8

THEY LET THEIR HORSES HIT A STEADY LOPE. THEY rode in silence, occupied by their own thoughts.

Slowly, Red Lake—misnamed, because it was

usually sky-blue—moved abreast of them, and then astern. The stirring of the hot morning wind brought a glitter of diamonds to its face. Castle Dome's bald head was white in the clear sunlight. The gaudy bluffs of the Vermillion Hills began to lift far in the distance to the north as they advanced beyond the shoulder of the dome.

These were the familiar landmarks of Del's past. The land, at least, had not changed. Graze seemed adequate. Filaree and grama were doing well in the swales. Mesquite in the gullies and along the drying streambeds promised good pod forage.

This gave way to coarse bunch, rabbit bush, prickly pear, and Spanish dagger as the horses settled to a grunting walk on the long, hot climb to Pancake Mesa.

Del had noted the scarcity of stock on the lower range, all of which should have been grazed by Two Star cattle. He had spotted a few head in that brand, but far from the numbers the range was capable of supporting.

The trail carried them to the flat expanse of the mesa. Walsh Camden had built windmill tanks here to pump water in the lush days when he had worked every inch of range and utilized every scrap of forage for raising beef and horses.

The two tanks they passed were dry and neglected, banks broken by rainstorms, and drying bottoms fouled by dead reptiles and small animals.

Two Star headquarters came in sight in the distance as they descended the east trail from the mesa. The whiteplastered walls of the sprawling adobe structure gleamed in the sun, and its red-tiled roof formed a brilliant U-shaped design, flanked by its lesser buildings and its corrals, and its hundreds of acres of fields cleared for irrigated haying.

But only a small portion of the hayfields was green with the season's first crop. As they rode nearer, Del became aware of decay and vacancy. The walls of the ranchhouse needed patching and repainting. The west wing had boarded windows. Varnish had weathered from the pillars and beams of the gallery that stretched the length of the face of the structure.

It had been a rare day in the past when Walsh Camden had sat down to supper with less than a dozen guests. All passersby had been welcome at Two Star for food and shelter as long as they cared to remain. All except the Kittridges.

Del recalled many lonely nights as a youth when be had sat on his horse in the darkness, listening to the music and laughter and the sounds of conviviality in the Camden household. His parents had never known about those secret pilgrimages alone into forbidden territory, never had known how desperately he had longed again to set foot inside the Camden house, where, as a boy, he and his parents had been so often entertained, and were now cast out.

Now, he was returning to the envied place in the hour of its sunset. Its glory was faded. The winds of misfortune were blowing dust around its empty corrals.

The majority of the outer buildings, which formed a sizable spread, seemed deserted. A crew house evidently was partly occupied. A few cow ponies grazed in a pasture. Del judged that Two Star was carrying no more than three or four riders. There had been a time when the regular crew numbered more than a score, with up to triple that number working calf brand and beef gather.

An aging, colored houseman came hurrying to take

the bit chains of the horses the women were riding. Maggie Riley emerged from the main door of the house.

"Thank you, George," Harriet Camden said as the houseman helped her down.

"Now where you-all been, ma'am?" George complained querulously. "I been frettin' about you'n Miss Kathryn clearin' out o' here 'afore sunup, without leavin' no word as to whar—"

He broke off, stammering, peering nearsightedly at Del who had remained mounted, awaiting the invitation to alight.

Kay Camden had dismounted. She handed the reins to George and spoke to Del. "Please join us in the house, Mr. Kittridge."

"Kittridge?" George gasped. "Dave Kittridge. I couldn't believe my eyes. Dat debbil, he come alive agin. I knowed he never was really dead. Lawd have mercy on us. He came back to ha'nt—"

"Nonsense!" Harriet Camden said. "This Kittridge might be a devil, but he's no ghost. He's very much alive."

"For the moment, at least," her niece said unsmilingly.

Del had been aware of a rhythmic drumming sound in the background. This ceased. Quinn Camden appeared from a wagon shed and stood staring disbelievingly.

He had stripped off his shirt and wore rubber-soled canvas shoes and had on fingerless, chamois gloves. The plated muscles of his chest and shoulders glistened with sweat, Del realized that the sound he had heard had been that of Quinn, working out on a punching bag.

Quinn came striding, glaring. "What'n hell's this?"

"Are you training for a fight, Quinn?" Del asked. "It's a mighty smart idea. You're going to have one."

"Any time," Quinn snarled. "How about now?"

"There are other things to be taken care of first, I regret to say," Del said. "It won't be with loaded gloves the next time. But it'll be only one round again. Maybe a long one like the last time. Maybe a short one."

Harriet Camden spoke. "So it was Quinn you fought. What started it?"

Kay Camden answered before anyone else could speak. "They had a little trouble in town yesterday, but it's all over."

"It's not quite over," Del said.

"What's Kittridge doing here?" Quinn demanded of his mother. "I never thought that you, of all persons, would—"

"Put on a shirt and come to the house," she said curtly. "You look positively indecent, Quinn. We are going to have a talk."

"A talk? With this fellow? Are you loco?"

She mounted the step to the gallery and motioned Del to follow. "Is Cullen home, Maggie?" she asked the housekeeper. "If so, I want him to join us."

"Sure an' he's home," Maggie sniffed. "But I don't know if he will take kindly to bein' waked. 'Twas daybreak when he arrived. An' him goin' to his bed with his boots and spurs on. The scut! He was still snorin' up a storm when I last listened at his door."

"Wake him up!" It was The Lady who was now speaking.

Quinn laughed derisively. He raised his voice so that it could be heard all over the spread. "Cullen! Cullen! Shake a leg. Your mother wants to talk to you. She and Del Kittridge!"

Harriet Camden led Del and her niece into the house. "Take care of the gentleman, George," she told the houseman. "Bring him, first, beer, if there is ice and it is cold. And then food. And don't waste time, staring like a toad. You heard what I said. Kathryn and myself will join Mr. Kittridge in Mr. Camden's office as soon as we change and freshen up."

" 'Tis meself that will see to it that the gentleman is fed an' cooled with beer," Maggie Riley said, " 'Twill be a pleasure."

Del sat in an oak-beamed room with thick white adobe walls that was Walsh Camden's business office at the ranch. A wide walnut table served as a desk. Letters and papers, neatly stacked, were gathering dust, awaiting the owner's return. Chairs of time-polished walnut stood beneath shelves containing pamphlets and volumes devoted to stock-raising and marketing information that extended back for years. Dry, practical statistics. Walsh Camden apparently had let the sun of joyful living die out of his life and had devoted himself to these arid subjects.

He drank the iced beer and ate the food that Maggie Riley brought on a silver tray. It was all delicious.

He arose as Kay and her aunt entered. They had changed to cool cotton dresses and slippers and had brushed their hair. Maggie brought iced tea and food for them.

Bootheels clumped on the polished tile of the hall. Quinn entered. He had donned a shirt and saddle boots. Also a gunbelt with a filled holster.

Del looked at the six-shooter. "You're packing unnecessary weight, Quinn," he said. "When I come at you, it won't be with a gun."

He added: "Unless you want it that way."

"Either way will be all right with me," Quinn said.

His mother spoke peremptorily. "Stop this sort of

99

talk! This is not a time for personal grudges."

She motioned Quinn to a chair, but he preferred to only plant a boot on it and remain standing. He began rolling a cigarette. "Make it short," he said. "Whatever reason you have for bringing a Kittridge here will have to be a mighty good one, Mother dear."

Shuffling steps sounded, and Cullen Camden appeared. He was unshaven, his eyes bloodshot. He swayed a trifle. He was barefoot, but had pulled on whipcord riding breeches and a double-breasted plaid shirt that he had worn in the parade the previous day.

"Bring him a stiff drink of whiskey, Maggie," his mother said. "Then take the bottle away and hide it."

"Ha-ha!" Cullen jeered. "I've got my own booze supply cached where I can lay my hands on it in a hurry, mother of mine. There's no need to—" His bloodshot eyes had focused on Del.

He swayed closer, blinking. "By God, it looks like him!" he mumbled. He peered at Quinn for confirmation.

"It's not a pink elephant you're seeing, brother," Quinn said. "It's a cattle thief in the flesh. A Kittridge."

"Sit down, Cullen," Kay said gently. She took his arm and steered him to a chair.

"*Gracias*, cousin," Cullen mumbled, and became meek and obedient in her hands.

Harriet Camden said, "Thank you, Maggie. Thank you, George. We'll call you if you're needed."

The housekeeper pushed George out of the room and closed the door behind them.

"This will be brief," Harriet said. "There's no time to be wasted. Your father's life is in danger. He is being held a prisoner in Mexico by Juan Torreón."

"A prisoner?" Quinn exclaimed. He wheeled on Del.

100

"Is that why you're here? You were one of Torreón's outfit, so I understand. I heard that you had ratted on him and—"

"Be quiet," his mother said. Briefly, she told of the message Del had brought of Walsh Camden's situation. She did not mention Marco Gonzales or the reason for his visit to Combabi.

The brothers sat staring as they listened. The hair-of-the-dog treatment that his mother had used had helped Cullen. The drink had cleared his head. He heard his mother out without interrupting, but kept snorting in disbelief.

Quinn uttered loud, rough laughter when she had finished. He slapped a hand on his thigh. "So, the old wolf's got his tail in a crack. Serves him right for dickering with a ladrón like Torreón."

"What do you intend to do, Mother?" Cullen asked.

"Round up every head of sound saddlestock we own." she said. "And as fast as humanly possible. If we're short of the three hundred, we'll buy horses to make up the difference."

"Buy?" Quinn jeered. "With what, Mother dear? Aren't we broke? Dead broke?"

"I've made arrangements to mortgage what we have left, if need be," she said quietly. "It happens that I have some property and money in my name."

Quinn scowled at her. "So! Did you hear that, Cullen? It seems that we've been left out of some of the family secrets. Weren't we led to understand that Two Star had exhausted all of its financial resources and that we were about to be cast out on the cold, cruel world to make our own livelihoods? Now we learn that we were not exactly as hard up as represented."

"Quit making speeches," Del said. "Juan Torreón's

no patient man. I'd say your father's got maybe a week to live unless someone shows up across the line with three hundred head of horses. Maybe ten days, if Torreón knows the horses are really on the way."

"What's that to you? Are you drawing cards in this game too? Your luck won't be any better than it was the other night at the Canary Cage."

"Nevertheless, I'm buying in," Del said.

"By whose invite?"

"By my request," his mother said. "And we must start on this at once. Today."

Quinn scowled at Del. "You don't expect me to believe you'd turn a hand to help my old man, do you? Not after what he did to the Kittridges. What's in it for you?"

"Let's just say I have mercenary motives," Del said. "I fight men who wear loaded gloves. I take a chance on 'dobe walls. I need money. Your mother has promised to pay me half of what Torreón has promised to fork over for the horses if I get them through."

"It's your funeral," Quinn said. "All anyone will be paid with down there is a bullet. You know that. You must know Juan Torreón."

"It *is* possible, of course, that Torreón might let your father go if the horses are delivered, regardless of whether he pays money for them," Del said. "In fact it's almost a sure thing. Walsh Camden, dead, would be worth nothing to him. How about looking at it that way?"

"I still say it's your funeral," Quinn snapped.

"And possibly yours."

"Meaning what?"

"I doubt if you're bulletproof, Quinn. Not even fistproof, as I aim to make sure when the sign is right.

102

Nor is your brother. As of now, you two are members of the Kittridge Long Riders. Temporarily, of course. The only members, maybe, outside of myself. The tomb might be empty when we try to open it. Likely the Long Riders will prefer to stay there."

Quinn uttered another of his bellows of derisive laughter. But it was a forced effort. "What are you raving about, Kittridge?"

"I understand that you two are going with me into Mexico," Del said. "At least your mother hopes so. Or do you have other ideas? Do I see the yellow coming to the surface?"

Quinn lunged at him, a fist clenched. But Kay moved in and blocked his path. "Stop it!" she said. "There's no time to fight among ourselves. Don't be a complete dunce!"

"I'm afraid it's a little late to change that," his mother said curtly. "Now stand there quietly, Quinn dear, and just listen. We can't waste more time in quarrels. Mr. Kittridge is to be in charge of running the horses into Mexico. You and Cullen are to follow his orders to the letter. It's our best hope of ever seeing your father alive again. Our only hope, I fear."

Quinn uttered a snort. "The old man got himself into it. Let him squirm his way out of it. He ought to have known better than try to whipsaw a man like Juan Torreón. If Kittridge wants to risk his neck for money to go down there, that's his worry. I'm staying out of it. It's a fool's errand anyway. He can't get away with it. Nobody can."

His mother was scarlet with shame. "This is your own father we're talking about. Your own flesh and blood. For once, you're going to act like a Camden."

"What did he ever do for me, except lambaste me

with a cane when I didn't walk soft around him and address him as sir? As far as I'm concerned, he can stay there and rot!"

"You can't mean that, son!"

"I can mean it, and do!" Quinn glared at Del. "To hell with you, Kittridge. To hell with everybody!"

He stomped out of the room and out of the house. Cullen arose, refusing to meet his mother's eyes.

Kay spoke bitterly. "Follow your big brother, Cullen. You're afraid too. Your father used the cane on you also. You owe him no help now. Put your tail between your legs and go with Quinn. Get drunk again."

She added grimly, "But be back tomorrow, sober and in shape to ride."

She turned on Del. Her lips were ashen with shame and humiliation. "There will be Camdens to ride with you," she said. "That's a promise."

Del shrugged. "Maybe. So, let's get down to business."

Cullen had paused. He stood there, at cross-purposes, trying to make up his mind.

Harriet Camden was trying her best to maintain her proud poise, but slow tears coursed down her cheeks. She spoke tiredly, "Just where do we start?"

Del did not answer for a time. He dragged his chair to the desk and sat with his arms resting on its edge, frowning as he stared, preoccupied, at Harriet Camden opposite him. But he was not really seeing her. This was his first chance to work out some plan of action.

Kay also drew her chair to the desk. She and her aunt waited in silence. Cullen continued to stand in indecision for a time. Finally, petulantly, he sat down again, glaring challengingly at Del's back.

"You'll take care of rounding up your saddlestock?"

Del finally said to Harriet. "How many do you figure you can tally up in a hurry? These horses have got to be in good shape. Nothing under four-year-olds."

She nodded. "I don't look for any difficulty on that score. Horses are about our only asset. Liability, rather. The market has been so bad the past year or two they don't bring enough to meet shipping costs. I sent the riders out this morning to start bringing them in from the range down around the mesa. We're carrying only three hands now. I'm sure Quinn and Cullen will help. We should know by tomorrow about how many animals we can muster."

"Everybody in the Combabi will know in a day or two that Two Star is rounding up horses," Del said, rubbing his chin. "There's got to be a reason for shaping up a market herd."

"Yes. Kay thought of that also. Last night. We mentioned to several persons in town, including Ed Donally, that we expected to close a deal in a day or so for the sale of a sizable bunch of horses to the Army for delivery at Fort Griffin."

Del grinned and eyed Kay approvingly. "You seem to be as fast with your thinking as you are on the draw. That must have set the tongues wagging. News like that spreads fast."

She did not unbend. If anything, the humiliation she had endured from Quinn's attitude had made her more distant. "We sent a rider to Griffin City this morning with a copy of a message he is to send by Western Union, addressed to my uncle," she said. "The telegram will read something like this: 'Preliminary contract approved for delivery of three hundred head of saddlestock. Advise placing horses on trail at once.' "

"Smart move," Del said. "Very smart."

"It will be signed with the name of Major Williams," she said. "There is no such person at Fort Griffin, as far as we know. We don't actually say we have a deal with the Army."

"But you'll let anyone who hears about the telegram draw their own conclusions," Del said. "Who was the man you sent to Griffin City?"

"Old Hy Slater. He's been with us for years. He won't talk."

"But you figure that the brass pounders *will* talk."

She smiled a little. "I doubt if anyone in Combabi ever got a telegram that wasn't public property before the day was out. Such things always leak out."

"I must take off my sombrero to you once again," Del said. "I believe you've taken care of a problem that had me winging. The bait will be swallowed. It's what is known as directing attention to the right hand so that they won't know what the left hand is up to. Nobody will be unduly curious about the destination of the horses if they happen to see them heading downcountry."

He got to his feet. "Let me know by tomorrow night how you come out with the gather."

Cullen spoke. "How are you going to get three hundred head of stock across the line? Border hopping's a lot tougher than it used to be, now that the Army's taking a hand."

"I haven't the slightest idea," Del said.

"What do you mean, you haven't the slightest idea? You Long Riders—"

"I never ran a steer or a loose horse across the line in my life," Del said. "Maybe I'll find out how it's done. If I'm lucky. Maybe both of us will learn. I understand that you're going with us whether you want to or not."

106

He turned to leave. Kay followed him. "When will we hear from you?"

"Tonight, I hope," he said. "I'm starting to do a little rounding up on my own part. It might be a little tougher than shaping up a bunch of horses. I'm going to try to bring the Long Riders back to life."

He added: "I doubt if they want to be resurrected."

Del walked out of the house and to where George had tethered his horse in the shade of the wagon shed. Inside the structure he could hear the steady rumble of the punching bag being pounded savagely.

Kay came to the door, watching in silence as he rode away. Back of her, in the shadows, he made out the face of her aunt, also watching. It occurred to him that the older woman had at least one strong arm on which to lean. There was not only one proud Lady Camden at Two Star, but two.

CHAPTER 9

THE BLAZE OF MIDAFTERNOON LAY STIFLINGLY ON Combabi when Del dismounted in the wide doorway of Rezin Bartee's blacksmith shop. Heat was reflected from the walls of the buildings and from the powder-dry dust of the street, and the residents of the town were mainly at siesta. Rezin's forge fire was banked, and he had been dozing in a barrel chair. The newly repaired wheel of a freighting wagon, bearing a fresh patch of felloes and spokes stood on the jacked-up axle of the vehicle in the rear yard.

Rezin awakened as Del swung down. "Act like you're looking at a loose shoe on my horse," Del said.

"That means you bring trouble," Rezin grunted. He

donned his leather apron and pretended that he was examining the front shoe of the steeldust. "I expected it," he added.

"I've agreed to run three hundred head of horses across the line," Del murmured.

"Gawdamighty!" Rezin breathed.

"How many of the old bunch can you get in touch with in a hurry?"

Rezin gave him a glare. "Do you know what—?"

"Yes. I know what I'm asking. There could be money in it for them. As much as fifteen thousand dollars for them to split up." He added: "I want no part of the money."

Rezin gave him a long look. "Maybe money wouldn't mean much to them either," he said. "Not that kind o' money."

Del related the facts, Rezin kept grunting in amazement. "They'll likely put a bullet in me if'n I ask 'em to go back to border hoppin' to help Walsh Camden," he growled. "They got no more use fer Walsh than a pot-hound has fer a skunk."

"It's Amata Villareal I'm asking this for," Del said. "And her child." He added: "And also as a personal favor."

Rezin stood snorting and mumbling to himself. "Damn you!" he finally growled. "You know danged well they can't turn you down. They was wild ones, reckless as colts an' mighty quick on the shoot in their day. But they always was suckers for things like this. They know about the Señora Villareal."

"They do? How—?"

"I told you once before that you hear all sorts of news in a blacksmith shop. We know all about her man who threw in with you when you made that lone-handed try to stop Juan Torreón. We were told that both you an' this Carlos Villareal might have squeezed out'n that trap you got into, except that you stalled for time so as to give the Señora and the niñita time to escape."

He wagged his head and said, "Your maw saved the bacon for the Long Riders one time when Walsh Camden had set a deadfall that would have caught us plenty tight. She swum the Combabi at night when the crick was in flood an' not fit for a fish. She got to us in time. Otherwise we'd have been shot to doll rags by Walsh Camden who was waitin' for us at a certain place with a bunch of gunmen."

He took off his smithy's apron, hung it on a hook and sighed. "They got a sentimental streak in them. Ever since that night the bunch sort of figured they owed considerable to womenkind in general. Money wouldn't interest 'em. The most of 'em have done pretty well since they quit listenin' to the hootowls."

"Where can you get in touch with them? How soon?"

Rezin gave him a twisted smile. "That's fer me to know. Where an' when do you want 'em to show up?"

"We've worked out a plan to make people believe the drive will head for Fort Griffin to fill an Army contract."

He told of the fake telegram that was to be sent. Rezin nodded. "I'll see to it that word o' the telegram gets around. Bill Dixon, the operator at the depot, is a friend o' mine."

The way he said it caused Del to eye him. "You don't mean that Bill Dixon was one of—?"

"I don't mean nothin' at all," Rezin said hastily. "Now you drag out o' here. Act like you got some store buyin' to do as a good reason for comin' back to town so soon. Folks know you're here. Not everybody's asleep. A pack o' gossipin' women are likely peekin' around the curtains right now, wonderin' what you're doin' in my shop, an' waitin' for you to come out."

He drew a wallet from his hip pocket and began peeling off bills. "Here's some money to pay for what you buy. Take it, blast you. It'll stand up as a good reason for you comin' back to town so soon. They wouldn't believe you rode all the way in, just to have a loose shoe nailed on your cayuse. Leave the horse here. I'll pretend to be workin' on it. When you come back I'll have a rifle an' a sixgun fer you. I got some extra ones in the house."

Del nodded and pocketed the money. "You win," he said.

He looked closer at Rezin. "Any particular reason?"

"For what?"

"For me packing iron out of town."

"Could be," Rezin said. "There's been a lot o' whisperin' in town since you pulled in yesterday. Some folks think you came to pay off the man who shot Dave Kittridge. Maybe this feller might take a notion to knock you off before you got him."

"Any ideas as to who might try the knocking off?"

"Nope," Rezin said. "If I knew, I'd take care o' him myself. Or some of us would. We thought a lot o' your paw. Get along with you now. See to it that the Camden horse drive holds over the first night at the haystack-shaped rock off the Fort Griffin trail this side o' the Cannon malpais."

Del nodded. "I know the place. Everybody does." He turned to leave, then paused. "What about Gonzales?" he asked.

"He's still in the jug here until the immigration boys can come up from El Paso an' take him under their wings," Rezin said.

Del left the shop and spent an hour buying the supplies a lone rancher might need, including tools for construction. He carried with him in a gunnysack enough food for a day or two and arranged with a freighter who would be heading for the Emeralds the next day to drop off the remainder of his purchases at the Rafter K fork off the main trail.

Returning to the blacksmith shop, he found his horse waiting, but Rezin was absent. A rifle and a Colt .45 were hidden in his tarp roll, along with boxes of shells. He rode out of town with the westering sun hot in his face. He looked back, wondering what secrets of the Long Riders were hidden back of the glinting walls of Combabi.

He let his horse set its own pace, for it was tiring. He throttled his own wild impatience for haste and followed the freighting trail westward as sundown came. He passed two town-bound freighters and overtook another who was outbound for the mines in the Emeralds.

He knew that all of this would be duly reported in town over the bars and at the supper tables, and at stopping points to the west. He wanted them to believe he was returning to his own land on Castle Creek.

But, once dusk concealed him, he left the freighting road and cut across country toward Two Star. He paused long enough to pull the rifle and the six-shooter from concealment. The rifle was a .44-40, long used, but in top condition. The Colt was accompanied by a holster and belt, both also having seen much wearing, but fit for efficient service. He buckled on the pistol and kept the rifle within quick reach in the tarp roll. Both guns had been cleaned and loaded by Rezin.

Only one or two window lights marked the location

of the Two Star spread of buildings in the darkness far ahead. He dismounted at a distance, watered his horse at the creek and tethered it. He approached the ranch on foot, circling wide of the outbuildings, for the chances were that some or all of the riders would have returned from the day's duties and would be awake in the crew quarters. If they discovered his presence they were sure to talk.

What lamplight there was in the main house came from rooms at the rear in the east wing. However, as he neared the step to the gallery, a voice spoke guardedly.

"All right. It's safe to come in."

Kay Camden arose from a porch swing which hung by chains from the gallery beams. He guessed that she must have been waiting there for a long time. Waiting for him to return.

He stepped onto the dark gallery. She laid a hand on his arm, steering him toward the door. "Aunt Harriet is awake and waiting," she whispered. "It will be better not to talk here. The riders are in the bunkhouse, but they might not all be asleep yet."

Del followed her down the unlighted, tile-floored hall to the door of a room that showed lamplight. Her aunt's voice responded when she tapped on the panel. She turned the knob and again took Del's arm, leading him into the room.

Harriet Camden, in a dressing gown, sat in an easy chair near a reading lamp with a knitting basket at her side. But there was no real attitude of repose in her. She paused knitting long enough to give Del a searching look, then forced her fingers to continue their mechanical task.

This was her bedroom—a large room, comfortably furnished, with rag rugs on the polished cedar floor. He

112

saw that recent events had taken toll of The Lady. She was drawn and tired and there was no color in her long, thin face. But she was making a determined effort to maintain her poise.

Her voice was precise in its diction and still coldly hostile. "I hardly hoped you could return so soon. I'm afraid such a short journey must mean bad news."

"That depends on the point of view," Del said. "I believe I've set the ball rolling. But that's about all I can tell you."

She and her niece brightened. "You mean you were able to get in touch with—with those you needed?" she asked eagerly. "So soon?"

"Something like that," Del said. "The next step is for you people to get the drive shaped up and headed toward Fort Griffin. The horses must be bedded the first night out at that big granite outcrop that looks like a haystack, just off the Fort Griffin trail, a mile or two this side of where the trail starts climbing into the rough country. Do you know the place I'm talking about?"

"Yes," Kay said. "Of course."

"Nobody is to know this except the three of us," Del said. "Nobody. Understand?"

Harriet spoke stiffly. "We understand. It's my sons you mean, of course. You don't trust them."

Del did not answer that. "What happens then?" she demanded.

"I don't know," Del said. "That will be decided by other men, perhaps."

"My sons will be there," Harriet Camden said. Her hands operated the needles angrily. Her thoughts carried her off into bitter distances.

Kay stroked her hair and brushed her cheek with her lips. "You must need rest, Aunt dear," she said. "Do you

113

want to turn in? Can you sleep?"

Her aunt smiled wanly and patted her hand. "Not yet, Kathryn. Later, perhaps. I'll sit up a while longer. You need not stay."

"Good night, ma'am," Del said, and he and Kay left the room.

She closed the door and they tiptoed down the hall to the open gallery.

"Thank you," she murmured.

Del was surprised. "For what?"

"For being kind to her. Kinder than she deserved. She, at least, believes in her sons. You could have hurt her by telling the truth about them. She knows the truth, but won't admit it."

She added, "I'm sorry you're involved in this. So terribly sorry. You have suffered enough and without reason."

Del peered at her. A waxing moon was still in the sky, but its faint light did not reach them in the shadow of the gallery. He could not read her expression, but he realized that, for the first time, he was touching the curtain that had separated him from the Camdens.

"Go on!" he said fiercely. "What are you trying to say?"

"I can't tell you."

His hand closed on her arm. "You can't go this far and then refuse to talk. Tell me!"

He was poignantly aware of her nearness, of her desirability, of her womanliness. He sensed that she was also very much aware of this new factor between them.

"What good would it do now?" she choked, and he saw that she was weeping. "Your father is gone. And your mother. Uncle Walsh has never really been alive for years. He's only been a ghost. A proud man who

114

believes he was betrayed by the only persons in life that he trusted. He's paid the price for blind pride. Just as Aunt Harriet has."

"I dont understand! What?"

"I didn't understand either until a few hours ago," she sobbed.

She pushed his hand away. "That's all I can tell you. I was taught to despise the Kittridges. By my uncle. I believed in him. Now I only pity him. He was mistaken. I want to tell him that. To his face. To make him know how wrong he was. It won't bring back the dead nor make up for the years of hatred and vindictiveness. But it might make it easier for him the rest of his life."

"You've got to tell—"

She moved away from him. "Our riders told us this evening they're sure we can round up at least three hundred head of sound saddlestock in another day or two. There'll be no need to buy from other ranchers."

"When can you people put them on the trail?"

"We hope by the day after tomorrow. I'll let you know. Where can I find you?"

"At Rafter K, laying out the foundation for a new house," he said. "That'll be for the benefit of anyone who might be keeping an eye on me, wondering if the Kittridge Long Riders might be listening again to the owls. I won't come back here. Anyone seen hobnobbing with me from now on will be tabbed for future reference by the law when it's learned that the Long Riders really did come back to life."

"I'm glad."

"Glad?"

"That you're going to build again at Rafter K. This time there'll be no hatred to tear it down. No misunderstandings. I promise that."

She added, "Good night!" and vanished into the dark hall before he could detain her for further questioning.

He left the gallery and headed across the open yard to return to his horse. He looked back at the house. Its peeling paint and scars of neglect were hidden in the silvery light of the moon. He was thinking of Kay Camden, picturing her walking down the tiled hall, picturing her grace and lithe straight-limbed way of carrying herself. He was remembering the softness of her voice, the warmth of her as he had touched her. She was strength and she was gentleness. She was determination and she was compassion. She was the real Lady of Two Star.

The loneliness that had always been a weight on him during the years of war and drifting since his father had followed his mother to the grave, was eased. The aimlessness of his life had faded. He suddenly felt that he was no longer alone. The future had a purpose. A shining, wonderful purpose. A promise of joy and fulfillment.

He tightened the cinches on his horse, which had benefitted by the rest, and headed for Castle Creek. He rode high in spirit. Around him the night had never before seemed so beautiful, so peaceful.

Juan Torreón's round, brown face, bronze-hard, rose in his mind. Sudden panic came. A fear of a kind he had never before known.

Life had never before seemed so priceless—and death so near. He now rode silent and taut in the saddle. The moon was ice cold, the land black and brooding.

The memory of Kay Camden's nearness was only that—a memory. And the future was only a wonderful dream from which he had awakened to face reality.

116

CHAPTER 10

HE BEGAN PREPARATIONS FOR THE NEW HOUSE THE next morning. Using the garden tools that he had found in the shed near the cemetery plot, he located the plowed-under foundation rocks of the original house.

At noon, he heard a gunshot in the distance, and saw the dust of a freight wagon on the main trail. Saddling up, he rode to the fork and found the supplies and implements he had bought the previous day.

With this better equipment, the task went faster. He was busy with a shovel and a crowbar at midafternoon when Marshal Thane Overmile rode across the creek.

The marshal dismounted and looked around. "I'd say that you aim to stay permanent," he said. "Only high ambition would drive a man to swing a shovel on a day like this."

"This time work is a pleasure," Del said.

"I rode out with a piece of information, even though my jurisdiction ends at town limits," Overmile said. "We had a bust-out at the jail last night. Marco Gonzales threw a gun on me while I was on duty, lettin' the turnkey go home for his supper. He had me dead to rights. He left me locked up in my own jail, an' ain't been seen since. The turnkey let me out when he got back from eatin'. A citizen said he recollected seein' a couple o' riders in the street about that time that was strangers. They're likely the ones that passed the gun to Gonzales. The citizen allowed that the two he saw probably might have been Mex, though they wasn't dressed like it. Must have been some of Juan Torreón's outfit. Gonzales likely didn't sneak across the line alone."

117

They eyed each other. Del laid aside the shovel and walked to where the rifle that Rezin had given him hung from the limb of a willow, along with the .45 and belt. He buckled on the pistol and returned, placing the rifle within close reach.

"I felt naked, sudden-like," he remarked dryly.

Overmile's smile pinched the sun wrinkles at the corners of his blue eyes and straight mouth. "From what I gather, Gonzales will never rest easy as long as you're alive."

"He sold me out to Juan Torreón's firing squad," Del said. "Me and a man I'd rode the river with."

Overmile nodded. "So I've heard. Carlos Villareal, wasn't it? I can savvy why a man like Gonzales might want to dust you. Well, it ain't likely he'd try it in daylight, but I wouldn't say about after dark. I don't know how well acquainted he is with this country, but he wouldn't have much trouble finding Rafter K, if he's got any friends in the Combabi. Everybody knows you're here. It's been a big sensation. If I was you, I'd sleep somewhere tonight where nobody can Injun up on you."

He mounted his horse to leave. "But who am I to give such advice to Dave Kittridge's son?" he remarked. "But Rezin thought I better ride out here to make sure you know the score."

Del stared disbelievingly as Marshal Overmile rode away. "It can't be," he finally muttered. "It just can't be!"

He resumed the physical struggle with the hot soil and the fire-blackened foundation stones. The task had its compensations. There was a vast measure of satisfaction in laboring on his own soil. This land was his. These were the same foundation stones his father

118

had blasted from the Castle Dome cliffs and hauled by wagon to this spot.

Here, in daylight, the uncertainties of life that had beset him the previous night seemed less foreboding, easier to deal with.

But when dusk came, the phantoms returned. Marco Gonzales had now joined that contingent. He cooked his meal over a tiny fire and finished it long before twilight had deepened into night.

He built the fire brighter. He had bought a new denim saddle jacket in Combabi, along with two white cotton shirts and socks and other items, as well as a quilt and blanket. He rigged the saddle jacket on dry sticks, and leaned it against a boulder near the fire, and his hat atop the lure. He retreated into the brush with the rifle and six-shooter and lay there silently for a long time.

But the fire burned low and the only sounds were the crickets and the stir of the willows in the night breeze. He finally returned to the camp, rolled the effigy in a blanket and left it there, while he made his own bed with the tarp and quilt at a distance.

He awakened often to listen, but as the night advanced, his vigilance relaxed. He doubted that Marco Gonzales would linger on this side of the line in order to attempt to kill him. The risk to Gonzales would be greater than the game, for he was a fugitive, with every person who sighted him being a potential danger.

He awakened suddenly and lay steel-taut. He felt that he had been asleep far too long and far too soundly. He could hear nothing tangible. Yet he was sure something had awakened him.

The morning star was blazing in the east. The moon, a half disc, was low over the western horizon. The locusts were rasping out their chorus with mechanical precision. This familiar beat faded. Then it resumed. And faltered again.

It had been this small departure from the ordinary that had awakened him. Something was moving in the brush, but at a distance from where he lay.

He reached for his rifle. Before be found it, a gun opened up beyond the creek. The reports came in a steady roar as the magazine was emptied.

He could hear bullets raking his camp which lay in the full light of the moon. Slugs were smashing into the blanketed scarecrow he had left there and chewing into earth and willow trunks.

He came to his knees, the rifle in his hands. He sent two bullets through the brush. He shouted and began running, but was blocked by a thicket.

The bushwhacker was fleeing. He could hear the crashing of brush in the darkness, but there was no way of knowing exactly the direction from which the sound came.

He circled the thicket, but was impeded by more obstacles. The echoes of his own efforts covered any sounds his quarry might now be making.

He pulled up and listened. Silence. Utter silence. He decided his man was crouching somewhere, immobile, waiting for him to make a move.

He began advancing again, pretending great stealth, but making sure the other would be aware he was on the prowl. War had taught him that attack was the best defense. It placed the weight of waiting and the fear of the unknown on the opponent.

He also was sure he had one other advantage over Marco Gonzales—if it *was* Gonzales there in the shadows. He knew the terrain. He knew the creek and its meanderings and just where were the paths made by cattle and deer and men. Gonzales would be handicapped, not only by this lack of knowledge, but by not knowing the easiest paths of escape, and there were a dozen routes by which a man who knew the area could withdraw with ease and speed.

The silence went on and on. Del continued advancing cautiously. As time passed, he moved more freely. Eventually, he was sure of it. His quarry had escaped. The brush was vacant except for himself.

Dawn was lighting the sky. When full daylight came, he searched the thickets thoroughly. His quarry evidently had known his way around, after all, and must have crept away immediately after shooting up the camp. No doubt he had left a horse at a distance and was miles away by this time.

He found the spot from which the bushwhacker had fired. He picked up five empty shells from among the dead willow leaves. They were .44-40s, like the ones in his own rifle which Rezin had given him. There were scores and probably hundreds of rifles in the Combabi that fired that same type of shell. He compared the marks of the firing pin with those on the two empty cartridges his own weapon had fired, and it was obvious they were so identical they offered no hope of betraying their source.

He kept searching, and finally found a place where a horse had been tethered for hours. The spot was nearly a mile from the creek. It had been ridden to the freighting trail but two jerkline teams and wagons had already passed by on the trail by the time Del had traced his quarry there, and all other hoof marks had been obliterated.

He retraced his way. It was past mid-morning by that time, and he had wasted hours without result. He was sure of only one thing in his mind. The man who had tried to murder him had not been Marco Gonzales. Whoever the intruder was, he had been exceedingly familiar with the area. Almost as familiar with it as Del himself.

Heading on foot back through the brush, he again came to the spot where the shots had been fired. And now he saw something that he had overlooked previously. A small tan-colored object lay partly trampled into the leafmold.

He picked it up, shaking the earth from it. It was a fingerless, chamois glove, the knuckles considerably scuffed by use.

He stood staring at his find and in his mind was the memory of a man emerging from the wagon shed at Two Star where he had been punching a boxing bag. Quinn Camden had been wearing fingerless chamois gloves to protect his hands.

Del tried on the glove. It fitted exactly. That meant that it probably would fit Quinn also.

He stood staring at the glove with bitter distaste. Quinn knew that he meant to settle, sooner or later, for the trickery in the boxing ring. It was in keeping with Quinn's nature that he would try to avoid fighting on even terms, apparently even to the point of attempting murder.

He pocketed the glove and returned to his task with the pick and shovel. He toiled through the day, and no visitors came. However, he knew he was being seen by freighters on the trail. They were usually equipped with field glasses or telescopes. They were the newspapers of the range and be was sure that his activity at Rafter K would be duly reported up and down the country.

When dusk came, he scouted through the brush in

122

search of a new, safe sleeping place. He halted, hearing the approach of a rider. The horse splashed across the creek in the moonlight. Kay Camden's voice called softly, "Where are you?"

Del walked into the open, the rifle slung under his arm, the pistol holstered at his hip.

She dismounted and looked at the weapons. "Trouble?" she asked.

"Someone shot up my camp last night," Del said. "They put a couple of bullet holes in a brand-new wool blanket. A waste of powder and lead, being as how I was bedded down elsewhere."

"That man Torreón sent," she exclaimed. "Marco Gonzales. We heard he had escaped from jail."

"No," Del said. "It was someone who knows the country and this particular spot of it mighty well."

He added, "Someone we probably both know."

She peered close at him. Her voice caught. "Quinn?"

"Do you know where he was last night?"

"At the ranch," she said. "Asleep. At least—" She halted, confused.

"At least he was supposed to have been there all night asleep," Del said. "But he also could have done a little moonlighting without anybody knowing he had left and come back."

"It just couldn't have been Quinn," she said shakily. "He's capable of many things, but I can't believe he's got the kind of courage, or whatever it takes, to do a thing like that."

Del drew the chamois glove from his pocket and handed it to her. "Whoever it was that tried to kill me dropped this as he was pulling out. I found it in the brush."

She was ashen. "Quinn wears gloves like that when

123

he's practicing his bag-punching," she said. "But there are other men who like that sort of thing too. They use fingerless glover, when they're roping cattle. All the dally-men do. Even some of the riders who come in from Texas with tie-down rigs."

She knew Del was well aware of these things. She was trying to keep talking, trying to find some way of exeonerating Quinn in her own mind. And failing. The dally-men she had mentioned were riders who preferred the Spanish- or California-style single cinch saddle, who threw a long lariat, and snubbed or "busted" cattle by taking a turn or two of the rope around the saddlehorn. Texans generally rode double-cinched saddles and swung a short rope that was tied to the horn.

"It's about Quinn's size," Del said. He added, "I'll try it on him one of these days, maybe."

He turned, pointing to the little cemetery, whose whitewashed fence posts stood out brightly in the moonlight. "Someone added a word to what I carved on my father's headstone. The word is 'murdered.' Who did it? And why?"

"It was placed there soon after you had left the Combabi," she said.

"You know who did it, but you don't intend to tell me."

"What good would it do now?" she asked wearily.

"It must have been put there so your uncle could see it. Was it the Long Riders who did it?"

"It was meant for my uncle, but it was not done by a Long Rider. And that's all I'm going to say."

She spoke again before he could ask another question. "The horses are ready. Three hundred and eight head. Aunt Harriet is allowing for death and accident on the trail. For hell and Gomorrah."

124

"Shove them on the trail at daybreak," Del said. "Remember what I told you about where to bed them tomorrow night."

"I remember," she said. "They'll be there."

"What about the telegram?"

"It came through. It's an open secret in Combabi by this time, no doubt."

"What happens when people find out that the horses never reached the fort? They'll know they were run across the line."

She shrugged. "I doubt if anything would push the reputation of the Camdens much lower in the Combabi. Even the ones who used to fawn on us are joining the pack to yap at us. Anyway, they'll have to prove that we're border hoppers."

She gave him a sidewise glance. "And from what I've heard of the Kittridge Long Riders," she said, "they leave no trail. They just pick up stolen cattle and vanish. I assume stolen horses are as easy to transport Do they have wings?"

"That, I doubt," Del said. "I suspect it isn't done with mirrors either, or that it's done easy. If you know any prayers, say them right steady for the next few days."

She extended a hand, "Friends?" she asked.

Del hesitated. He was thinking of Quinn. Her blood cousin. He took her hand, held it in his palm, and she let it lie there, He could feel the run of tension in her. "Friends!" he said.

She moved away suddenly and swung into the saddle. "Tomorrow night, then," she said.

"How many riders will be with the bunch?" he asked.

"Four," she said. "Quinn and Cullen and two more. You can trust them all."

She wheeled the horse and rode away at a lope. Del

returned to his camp. He selected what food he could carry on his horse and cached the remainder. He saddled up and stood for a space looking at the moonlit flat. Remembering dreams.

Then he mounted and headed for Combabi. He avoided the freighting trail, staying well out of sight and sound of it. There was always travel on it, even at night, and he particularly did not want to be seen on this ride.

It was past ten o'clock when he left his horse on the outskirts of town and entered on foot by way of side lanes. Rezin's blacksmith shop was closed, the swing doors padlocked. His living quarters in a small cottage at the rear were dark also, but Del's cautious tap on the rear door brought quick response.

Rezin admitted him into the unlighted kitchen which was heavy with the tang of pipe tobacco smoke.

"I been expectin' you," said Rezin, who was fully dressed. "Two Star's got the horses rounded up, ain't they?"

"Looks like I wasted a ride to town just to tell you something you already know," Del said. "How did you—?"

"I got ways o' keepin' track o' things."

"They'll hit the trail at daybreak," Del said.

"Keno," Rezin said.

Del waited. "Is that all you've got to say?" he finally demanded. "What about your side of it? Did you—?"

"I said, keno, didn't I?" Rezin growled irritably. "That's the part of it I wanted to know about. Who told you they was rollin' at daybreak?"

"Kathryn Camden. She came to my camp at dark. How many men will you—?"

"Enough to handle it," Rezin grunted. "We don't need a crowd. Not o' the kind o' men I'm bringin'. Now

126

you slope out o' here before some nosy neighbor wakes up an' gets to wonderin' about things. I swear, some o' these women here in Combabi try to keep cases on every move I make, day or night."

"It couldn't be because maybe some of your goings-on, day or night, in the past, might have puzzled them," Del commented. "You haven't gone to bed early every night in your life, my friend. Not by a long shot."

"Get along with you," Rezin said. "Show up at that granite haystack as close onto midnight as you can figure it tomorrow night. Don't be late. You'll hear the owls hoot."

"I'll show up," Del said, "unless I happen to bump into the same man who tried to pick me off last night."

"How's that ag'in?"

Del told of the attempted bushwhacking and described the chamois glove he had found. He did not mention that he was sure he knew the identity of the intruder. But Rezin wasn't fooled.

"What about Quinn Camden?" Rezin asked.

"What about him?"

"Don't try to play innocent with me. You're pretty danged sure in your mind it was Quinn that tried to ventilate you. Everybody who's ever been to Two Star has seen all that stuff in the shed that he uses to keep in shape for prize fightin'. I've seen it myself. An' I've seen him wearin' gloves just like this one when he was workin' out on the bag."

"Kathryn Camden says he never left Two Star last night."

"He could have sneaked out an' come back while she was asleep, most likely. He knows you intend to lock horns with him to pay off for usin' loaded gloves on you. You know as well as I do that it's a thousand to

127

one that he tried to settle your hash ahead o' time."

"It was pointed out to me that other people wear these kind of gloves. Lots of men do when they're roping."

Rezin was silent for a space. "I can guess who pointed that out," he said. "The same one what said Quinn never left the ranch last night. But you got to admit she's right. Can't hang a man on suspicion. Not 'til we're sure the glove fits, at least." He added sharply. "Is Quinn, goin' on the drive?"

"Kay Camden said he'd be with the horses, but I doubt it. He told his mother he didn't give a whoop whether his father ever got out of Mexico alive."

"It'd be better if he stayed clear," Rezin said. "This sashay is goin' to be ticklish enough, without the rest o' us havin' to worry about you two lockin' horns at a time when it might spill the coffee. How about the other one? Cullen?"

"Both Cullen and Quinn are supposed to go out with the drive, along with two other Two Star hands," Del said.

"That bunch o' horses," Rezin said, "are likely to find themselves bein' highballed along by a brand-new crew somewhere along the way. *Adios* now."

Del left the cottage quietly, made his way back to his horse and pulled out. He camped for the night half a dozen miles southeast of town.

After sunup, from a distance, he watched the long plume of dust that was being kicked up by a sizable band of horses that appeared from the direction of Two Star and moved steadily abeam, vanishing at mid-morning among the rolling hills to the east. The drive was paralleling the Fort Griffin trail.

He slept again until sundown on his tarp in the shade of brush. Despite the heat of the day he enjoyed the first solid rest he had gained in longer than he cared to try to remember. He ate a cold meal, topped off with a very satisfying tin of canned peaches, for he did not care to build a coffee fire that might arouse the curiosity of some passerby on the trail.

There was even the chance a Ranger might be in the Combabi. Another possibility, although remote, was that an Army patrol might decide to swing this far north, although the border, which was their normal beat, was nearly a day's journey to the south.

Of either of these hazards, an encounter with the Rangers was the danger most to be avoided. The Rangers, few in number, were all tough, hard-bitten, picked men, wise in the ways of the border and experienced in smelling out trouble. They might be suspicious of a lone rider who was avoiding the main trail, and likely would ask questions difficult to answer.

In addition, a Ranger would likely identify him as Dave Kittridge's son because of his resemblance to his father, and would become doubly suspicious.

When deep dusk came, he saddled and rode eastward, judging his pace so that he would arrive at his destination as close as possible to the midnight hour that Rezin had stipulated.

He had no watch, but he was adept at judging time by the stars, and was sure he was punctual when he sighted the rounded top of the rock outcrop that was shaped like a haystack.

He rode directly toward the landmark, abandoning all attempt at stealth. The outcrop rose fifty feet or more above its flat surroundings. The base was undercut and weathered and surrounded by thickets that were fed by a spring that flowed from beneath the rock.

The brush was interlaced with cattle and game trails

and the ashes of many campfires blackened the numerous small clearings. This landmark had been a meeting place, a shelter from storms and at times a fortress for men, red and white, far back into time.

His horse pricked its ears and snuffled. He dismounted and stood waiting. Presently, a voice spoke from the shadows of the rock ahead. "This way, Kittridge."

Del led his horse closer. He could make out the shapes of three more saddle mounts and of the three men who were waiting.

"Right on time, Kittridge," said a voice that was familiar.

Del peered. He moved closer to make sure. "No!" he exclaimed.

"Yes," the man said. He was Jim Shanahan, owner of the Canary Cage in Combabi.

Del looked at Shanahan's companions. And had another shock. One was a stranger, but the other was not. "So that's how it is?" he said disbelievingly.

"That's how it is," said Thane Overmile, town marshal of Combabi. "I thought you had guessed it the other afternoon when I came to tell you about Marco Gonzales bustin' jail."

"The thought crossed my mind and just kept going," Del said. "I just couldn't believe it."

"I was a Kittridge Long Rider before I wore the badge," Overmile said. "So was Jim. But here's one you haven't met. Tucson, this is Dave Kittridge's son, Del. Del, this is Tucson Slim."

"I've heard of Tucson Slim," Del said.

They shook hands. Like Overmile, Tucson Slim was a lean, leathery man of perhaps forty, quietly garbed in a dark cotton shirt, black vest, trousers stuffed in the tops of cow-boots. He carried a six-shooter on his left side.

Tucson Slim was a southpaw. And deadly in a gunfight. He had been a law officer in tough mining camps in the Emeralds and before that, Del recalled he was said to have been a young cavalry lieutenant, and had fought in the plains wars when the Sioux and Cheyenne were still riding.

"Slim happened to drop into Combabi yesterday to have a drink with some of us old sidekicks of his," Thane Overmile explained. "He was on his way to San Anton' to take a job as troubleshooter in a big saloon, but this sounded more to his likin', so here he is."

Rezin arrived, along with another man. This one was a surprise to Del also. He was the dour, saturnine Tim Buttons, the livery owner with whom he had clashed over the price of boarding his horse.

Buttons bobbed his head in Del's direction as he dismounted. "You didn't expect to find out I was one of the bunch too, did you?" he asked. " 'Specially after the way I acted when you first showed up."

"I understand," Del said,

"It was best not to act too friendly. If folks suspected I'd been one of the Kittridge bunch, it'd hurt my business. An' I ain't gittin' rich the way it is."

"You always was one to put business before pleasure, Buttons," Tucson Slim said curtly, then turned to Del and thrust out a hand. "You might think you never saw me before, but you did. I come to Rafter K, pretendin' to be a grubliner a couple of times, so as to bring some news to Dave about things we both was interested in. You was a wild young colt in them days. Me an' your father was mighty good friends."

A new rider appeared in the moonlight and Rezin called to him to join them. He was Leonard Willis, the

131

lawyer, who had cleaned Del out in the poker game at Shanahan's Canary Cage.

"Nothing surprises me any longer," Del said as he shook hands with the latest arrival.

"Sorry about that queen hand that I came up with," said Willis. "I like a man who backs his judgment to the limit. By all the odds of poker, you should have won that pot."

"I'm beginning to wonder if everybody in the Combabi was a border runner," Del said.

Willis laughed, "Most of them were, at one time or another. But not with us. We never rode with anyone but your father."

"We were Kittridge Long Riders," Tucson Slim said. There was quiet pride in his voice.

"Well, we're all here," said Rezin. "Len, you're late. Ten minutes or more. It's past midnight."

"Sorry," the lawyer said. "I had a client to take care of at the last moment and it took more time than I had expected."

Del saw that he was genuinely concerned. He turned to the others and said, "I'll be punctual from now on."

He explained to Del, "Exact timing is vital in matters such as this. Failure to meet commitments could be fatal to all of us."

"Won't Combabi wonder why some of its prominent citizens are all missing at the same time?" Del asked.

"Why should they?" Willis said. "Thane, here, is supposed to be testifying in a court case at Douglas. He's often away on such matters. I'm representing a client at Bisbee in a mining matter. At least as far as Combabi is concerned. Rezin and Tim Buttons are gone on a turkey hunt."

"Let's make tracks," Rezin said. "There's a bunch of

132

horses to be rustled, and we've got to be long gone with them come daybreak before a Ranger or an Army patrol comes snoopin'."

They tightened cinches and mounted. "I know of one poor devil who's going to be blessed with a bunch of saddle buffs before this is ended and his name is Willis," Len Willis said. "I've done most of my riding in a swivel chair these past few years." He eyed the others. "But, if misery loves company, as they say, I'll be one of the crowd. Jim, you don't look like you've built up any calluses on your bottom lately."

"I came prepared," Shanahan said. "I fetched along a jug of cure-all."

"About a hundred proof from old Kentucky, I hope," Rezin said.

"I could stand a snort right now," Tim Buttons spoke up eagerly.

"Likker always did taste better to you, Buttons, when you wasn't payin' for it," Tucson Slim said.

"The jug stays closed," Shanahan said. "You all know the rule. No drinking until the job is roped, thrown, branded, an' we're on our way back. Dave Kittridge made that rule and it was one of the best he ever set down. We couldn't afford befuddled minds in those days. We can less afford it now."

There were many questions Del wanted to ask. But he refrained, sensing that they would offer only what explanation they decided was necessary.

It was Tucson Slim who finally acted as spokesman. "We know you're right curious about this whole setup. Len, you sling words better'n any of us. You tell him."

"There's not too much to explain," the lawyer said. "There were other Long Riders, of course. Not too many at that. Dave Kittridge was choosy about who

133

joined up with him. He never cottoned to killers or those with raw owlhoot blood in them. Every Long Rider had his own motive, of course. Some rode for the adventure of it, some for profit. Neither kind stayed with it long. There was too much adventure and mighty little profit. The majority of us rode for the same reason your father did. We don't like to be stepped on, or to see others stepped on."

"We don't like little tin gods," Tucson said. "Whether their name is Walsh Camden or Juan Torreón. We rode long for reasons somewhat like the ones that sent you fightin' Torreón instead o' followin him."

"Tucson, here, had decided to settle down and try to raise cattle," Willis explained. "He put what money he had into a little brand in the Combabi just about the time Walsh Camden set out to smash your father. Tucson was wiped out in a hurry."

"Like a tumblebug," Tucson said. "I didn't last out the first summer."

"Rezin came under Camden's wrath because he and your father went into partnership in wagon freighting when they made that big silver strike in the Emeralds," Willis explained. "Camden spent a lot of money opening up a freight line of his own, and undercut prices so that Rezin was soon back in the blacksmith shop. In my case, he turned thumbs down on me because I refused to act as attorney for him. I didn't like his methods. He let it be known that anyone who hired me as their lawyer could expect nothing but bad luck from Two Star. That meant that any merchant would lose his biggest customer. So I became a Long Rider. But, better still, I was also lucky at poker."

"As I found out," Del said.

"As for Shanahan and our dashing town marshal—?"

134

"Just say we didn't like Walsh or his arrogance," Overmile said. "And that Dave Kittridge had done some big favors for us in the past, and we didn't like the way Walsh went after him."

"Also let's say we all was ten years younger an' sorta liked the spice o' danger," Rezin said dryly. "The Lord knows, that was the only thing any of us got out of it."

They rode on, stirrup-to-stirrup in the moonlight. Shanahan, Len Willis, and Overmile hung mainly together. Theirs was the bantering talk of old friends. Rezin joined them at intervals, then would gravitate back to the side of Del and Tucson Slim.

Del was discovering that he and the quiet, soft-spoken gunman had much in common. Both had soldiered and had seen battle action. This was a bond, but it went beyond that. Here, Del realized, was a man who would be a friend. Here was another one like Carlos Villareal.

Tim Buttons rode mainly alone, humped like a monkey in the saddle. He voiced querulous complaints occasionally, and Del came to understand that here was one Long Rider at least who would have preferred to let the past stay buried. Evidently Rezin had used considerable persuasion to induce the livery man to join the venture.

Buttons treated his horse as an adversary, never giving the animal its way, never letting it choose its own path or its own gait.

"I'm sayin' I was a fool to let you bamboozle me into this loco thing," Buttons finally burst out, glaring at Rezin. "What'n blazes do I keer if'n Walsh Camden is 'dobe-walled down there. Good enough for him, I say."

"I explained to you that it wasn't Walsh Camden we aim to help," Rezin said curtly. "We figure we owe it to the son of Lottie Kittridge to give him a little help. You was along the night we'd all have been wiped out, except for Lottie. So quit squawkin'. Also quit giggin' that *caballo* of yours around. Ride lighter on the bit. Do you want to sull that damned horse before we even get started?"

Buttons subsided. After that his horse had an easier time of it, for Rezin kept a close eye on its rider. Del became suddenly aware there was steel below the casual, velvet demeanor of these men he was riding with. These Long Riders.

They had their rules of discipline, and he realized it would go hard with any member who failed to heed.

CHAPTER 11

AFTER A TIME, REZIN, WHO WAS SCOUTING WELL AHEAD of the others, pulled up until they joined him. Del could now hear the intermittent clanking of a herd bell in the moonlight far ahead.

He made out the faint red dot of a lantern. It was a long rifleshot away and marked the location of the camp the riders had made well away from the bed ground of the Two Star band of horses.

"How many riders did you say?" Rezin asked Del.

"Two, in addition to Quinn and Cullen," Del said, knowing that Rezin was asking him to repeat this information for the benefit of the others rather than himself.

"Maybe Quinn an' Cullen yellowed out," Rezin grunted. "Chances are they're in town, ridin' the rail of a bar. Anyway, who will the other two riders be?"

"Kay Camden said they'd be men who we could trust."

Rezin turned to the others. "How about it?"

Jim Shanahan spoke. "I take it the young lady spoke for her aunt. If Harriet Camden says the men can be trusted, that's good enough for me. I can't say as much if it had been her sons' word. Or Walsh's."

There were nods of agreement. Except from Tim Buttons. "We could be steppin' into a deadfall," he protested. "Who knows but what this whole thing is a flimflam to find out who rode with Dave Kittridge in the old days."

Shanahan twisted in the saddle, glaring. "If you're that spooky, then wear that gunnysack, like you used to do," he said contemptuously.

"That's just what I aim to do," Buttons said. "An' so ought the rest of you. I don't trust nobody, nor do I take the word of Harriet Camden. If anybody recognizes any of us, an' talks, it's likely to mean a long jolt in prison for us."

"Cover your head, then," Shanahan said. "But that's not the Long Rider way and you know it."

Del intervened, seeing that the increasing friction might get out of hand. "There'll likely be two of them on night herd and two sleeping. Fact is, I can make out one rider over there on the right where the dead yucca stalks stand up on the skyline. And there's another off to the left."

He dismounted, tossing the reins to Rezin. "I'll scout the camp, There should be only two there. Wait here."

He moved in on foot until he reached a point where he could make out two figures on bed tarps in the lantern light and moonlight. Two night horses stood on picket, saddled and ready for quick service in case of emergency.

He returned to his companions. "All right. Only four

137

in all. I'm sure we're expected. Otherwise they wouldn't bother putting out a lantern on a moonlit night."

Buttons pulled a feedsack over his head, equipped with eye and nose openings. He had already donned a big, shapeless black slicker outside of which he had strapped a holstered six-shooter.

"Let's go!" Del said, swinging his horse in the direction of the lantern beacon.

Tucson Slim uttered a low, exultant, "Yippee!!"

"I'm ten years younger," Shanahan said. "I'm a curly wolf from Tennessee, ain't told the truth since the age o' three."

Shanahan's battle-scarred face was alight, a broad grin on his mouth. Thane Overmile and Len Willis rode high in the stirrups, smiling as though breathing air that was wine. Rezin's beard was thrust forward. He, too, wore that same wild, reckless grin.

Del had an eerie sensation that he had seven companions, not six. He felt that the others were aware of this also. Even surer of it than he. They believed Dave Kittridge was riding long with them once again.

Time had rolled back for them. They were once again border hoppers, risking their freedom, their lives in a dangerous contest. For he understood now that with them it had been a contest and not a way of life. It had been a battle against Walsh Camden and the things for which he had stood.

Once more, and for the last time, no doubt, they were together in a joust with danger. For this night, at least, the monotony of lawbooks was forgotten for Leonard Willis, and the heat and soot of the forge fire for Rezin. Jim Shanahan's gambling blood was racing to the challenge of a game in which there was no limit, even to life itself.

Tucson Slim's taciturn reserve had been shed away for the moment and he uttered a suppressed cowboy yell. For there were no pasts for them in this instant, no recollections, no regrets. They were young and wild and heedless again.

It came to Del that he was not only one of them, but that they were looking for him to lead them. He and the invisible one Harriet Camden had said he resembled so remarkably.

He accepted the assignment. He had led men in battle in the past. He knew the penalty, the terrible responsibility of leadership.

He led them into the lantern light. The two occupants of the camp were awake and alert in their blankets, as though they had been expecting them.

Del peered. He looked at his companions. They sat feeling foolish, the champagne flush fading.

The eyes that gazed up at them were those of women. Harriet Camden and her niece.

The two women got to their feet. They were fully dressed in dark riding habits, even to their boots.

Harriet gazed from face to face. "Len Willis," she said in her cultured voice, "You're one I never suspected. But I should have known. You were always the romantic one. As for Rezin, here, I never had any doubt but that he was a Long Rider. He was Dave Kittridge's best friend."

She eyed Jim Shanahan. "As for you, Jim Shanahan, if you still hold to your faith, you'll have something to really tell your priest at next confession. I've always felt that back of that Irish blarney there was a rogue. And I've always known that those goldpieces that appeared in the charity boxes of the Church of the Magdalene, the First Baptist Church, and the Methodist congregation

139

were from you, as the biggest share of the profits from rustled Two Star beef."

"I am admitting nothing, Harriet," Shanahan said, "nor confessing anything at this moment."

"It is a sin to try to buy your way into heaven," she said. "Especially with the money from stolen beef." She sternly eyed Thane Overmile. "A strange place for an officer of the law," she said.

"I enforce the law in town," Overmile said, "as I have done without fear or favor since I took the badge. There are times, however, when it is necessary to go outside the law. Justice is not only blind, but badly in error at times."

"My name's Tucson, ma'am," Tucson Slim said, in answer to her questioning stare, "Tucson Slim, they call me."

"Your name is no stranger to me or to anyone in the territory," she said. "I was never aware you rode with Dave Kittridge. The night is full of surprises."

She looked at the masked member of the party. "Take the sack off your head, Tim," she said curtly. "Learn to sit a horse like a man instead of an ape, if you don't want to be recognized."

Buttons sheepishly removed his mask. "I come here ag' in my better judgment, Mrs. Camden," he said.

"Who's night hawking?" Del asked.

It was Kay who answered. "Quinn and Cullen. We've been waiting for you to show up."

"Anyone else with you?"

"No. We decided it would be better to keep this all in the family. I told you there would be four riders with the drive. We are the four."

"You mean you two ladies have been working as—?" Len Willis began.

"Of course," Harriet said impatiently. "It isn't the first time I've filled in as a trail hand in emergencies. I know which end of the horse to hang a headstall on."

"That's for mighty sure," Rezin said.

"Time's wasting," Del said. He touched the brim of his hat. "You'll hear from us, sooner or later, ladies. *Adios*."

He led the way toward the bed grounds. Quinn and Cullen came riding to meet them.

The brothers stared at Del's companions. "Well, I'll be teetotally bogged down in gumbo and kissed by a coyote," Quinn exclaimed. His mouth shaped into an ugly twist. "Is this for sure, Kittridge? Don't tell me that some of our most prominent citizens got their starts riding long in the moonlight."

"That's how it is, Quinn," Del said. "And I might warn you that they don't like the way you're talking."

"So?" Quinn spat. "How am I supposed to talk in their presence? Am I to be respectful just became a bunch of cattle thieves go back to their old trade? Three hundred head of horses, with a ready market in Mexico, seems to be a temptation they couldn't resist."

Jim Shanahan, with a growl of fury, spurred his horse toward Quinn. Tucson Slim, faster and far more deadly, had already moved in ahead of him.

"You've got a gun on you, I see," Tucson said to Quinn. "Want to make a try for it, you pup. I'll—"

"He's mine," Del said. "I claim first crack at him. Get Rezin to tell you why. It's a story about a fight in a prize ring and loaded gloves. He's mine. But this is not the time. We've got other chores that come first."

That cooled them, brought them back to the business at hand. Tucson Slim turned away. Shanahan said, "I'll wait, but not forever."

141

Quinn tried to laugh—and failed. He had been near a gunfight with a man adept at that trade, and he suddenly was aware of his narrow escape.

Del looked at Rezin. "You'll ride pilot, of course."

Rezin nodded. He spoke to the Camden brothers. "If either o' you are thinkin' that you'll back out, it's too late. We can't leave anyone behind. You two will ride swing on left flank. Len an' Tim on right swing with Jim helpin' me at point. Thane, Tucson, an' Del can clean up."

Tucson sighed. "I always seem to end up pulling drag. I've swallowed enough dust from cow critters, horse critters, mule critters, and even human critters in my day to pave a wide highway to hell."

But he was pleased. Riding drag would be a task for tough, quick-thinking men. It would be their job to keep the horses moving in tight formation, with no bunch quitters left behind to give away the route they were taking. In case of trouble, it would be up to them to meet it head-on and give their companions a chance to organize for resistance or escape.

With nine men working them, the horses were swiftly crowded into motion. Swinging rope ends, the riders headed the animals eastward at a gallop. They kept the band running until the horses were willing to settle to an obedient trot.

Riding clear of the dust, Del peered ahead. Rezin seemed to be veering the drive southward toward the Cannon Mountains, a low, but extremely rough range. The Cannons were in reality a badlands, or malpais, an area of ridges and arroyos where vegetation was scant. Its yellow face basked in the sun in summer, for the formation was of clay and soft slate. Line fences barred stock from the Cannons, for the malpais could become a deathtrap of mud during storms, and its draws subject to raging flash floods. The Cannon River slashed through its heart in a gloomy ten-mile gorge—a barrier that made the Cannons impassable from north to south.

Tucson Slim joined Del briefly in order to gain a whiff of clear air. "I take it that Rezin knows he's heading straight for the malpais," Del commented.

"Yep," Tucson said.

"At this season? We've had a thunderstorm every afternoon. And there'll likely be more. We'll bog down in there."

Tucson chuckled. "I keep forgettin' that you never been on a run. You're goin' to think your hair has turned gray before many more hours. An' maybe it will at that."

Del stood up in the stirrups, peering. He again counted the riders in sight on swing and point ahead.

"And two makes seven," he exclaimed. "Instead of six."

He touched his horse and rode at a gallop along the left flank. There were three riders on swing on this side of the column of horses.

The third rider was Kay Camden. She wore saddle jeans, a dark cotton shirt, and a vest, and had a straw sombrero tied under her chin by a braided band. She had seen him coming, but she ignored him until he had yanked his horse to a stop alongside her mount.

"No, you don't!" he said angrily.

"Oh, yes indeed I do," she said defiantly.

"Where's your aunt?"

"Well on her way back to Two Star by this time."

"That's where you're going too."

"You're wrong. I'm staying with the drive."

"Why? And it better be a damned good reason."

"Haven't you been taught not to swear in the presence of ladies?"

"Let's hear why you're being mule-headed?"

She didn't answer for a moment. "To make sure that we keep our promise that at least some of the Camdens stand by their own flesh and blood and take their own chances in this thing."

She added before Del could speak, "Discussion ended."

Cullen came racing up, hurling his horse to an angry stop. Quinn was spurring toward them also. "Do you fools know where you're going?" Cullen raged. "That's the Cannon malpais ahead. Or hasn't anyone noticed?"

"What are you and Bartee trying to do, Kittridge?" Quinn yelled. "Lose three hundred head of horses for Two Star? You know what we'd be in for if we were caught by a big rain in that place. And hot nights like this are weather breeders."

He pointed to massive white clouds that lay on the horizon, lighted by the moon. "And that's what's being bred. Those are thunderheads or I never saw any."

"Take your complaints to Rezin," Del said. "He's piloting this drive."

"From what I gathered, you seem to be the ramrod," Quinn snapped, "Just what's the plan?"

"I wouldn't know," Del said.

"Wouldn't know? You mean nobody has any idea where we're heading? I thought you border hoppers knew secret ways of—"

"The sorry truth," Del said, "is that I've no more knowledge than you as to how, where, or when the bunch ran the border."

Quinn laughed jeeringly. "Don't try to make me believe anything like that, Kittridge!"

144

Rezin came riding up, having discovered the parley. He glared at Kay. She beat him to the draw. "I know what you're about to say, Mr. Bartee. However, I'm going with the run. That's final. Let's not waste time debating it."

Rezin shifted the stem of wild oats he was chewing. He inspected the horse she was riding. It was a solid-barreled bay gelding with one white stocking and a blaze on its forehead. "How's that cayuse in swimmin' water?" he asked. "It's got a sizable breadbasket. I like a horse that can carry plenty of air in its paunch when I ride a deep ford. Ever tried this one out in fast water?"

She patted the bay on the neck. "Yes. He's a real water dog."

"Good. We all better make sure we're on animals that know how to stay afloat. You two Camden brothers ought to know enough about your own cavvy to pick out good river horses for all of us."

"All Camden horses can take care of themselves in water," Quinn said. He was suddenly somewhat subdued. "Where do we do this swimming?" he asked cautiously.

"In the Cannon," Rezin said. "Where else? There ain't any other swimmin' water that I know of in eighty miles at this time o' year."

"In the Cannon?" Quinn echoed incredulously. "But—"

Rezin spurred his horse and loped back to his place at point. He waved an arm and yelled, "Crowd 'em! Roll their tails! Hike!"

Del eyed Quinn. "So now you know. Rezin forgot one item. He forgot to ask us humans if we could swim too. Can you?"

Quinn nor Cullen answered. They swung their horses

145

and rode away.

"They can't swim a stroke," Kay said.

CHAPTER 12

DAYBREAK WAS STILL AN HOUR AWAY WHEN REZIN raised an arm and fanned it in a circle. They threw the horses off to graze.

The moon, swinging low above the massive clouds on the horizon, was the color of old copper. On either hand, yellow clay buttes, eroded and veined by wind and rain of the past, rose eerily in tombstone silence, echoing the sounds the horses made as they competed for the scant forage.

Rezin had led the way through the malpais for two hours. They had now emerged onto this flat, which at times evidently was a temporary sink for the flash floods that swept out of the draws that converged here. The surface was of dried, yellow mud, heat-cracked and breaking into powder beneath the hoofs of the animals. Scant vegetation had found footholds on hummocks. Del knew that the main river could not be far ahead.

Rezin waited until daybreak. "All right," he said, pointing to Quinn and Cullen. "Point out the best swimmin' horses in the bunch, so we can cut them out for saddlin'. Len, you an' Thane rig ropes to corral 'em."

He added grimly, "If you're not sure about these horses, say so. We don't want any mistakes. Where we're goin', one mistake will be our last."

Quinn obeyed sullenly, but Cullen showed greater energy in selecting mounts from the herd. The animals they indicated were hazed into the rope enclosure that

146

had been set up.

Rezin sat by, restraining his impatience while the Long Riders passed critical judgment on the assortment, accepting some and rejecting others. When everybody was at least partly satisfied with their mounts, he said, "Rig with only headstalls, an' surcingles. Leave your saddles here. Bedrolls an' war sacks too, unless you're packin' mighty light. Thane will fetch all that sort o' stuff along later."

The men began complying. They pulled off their boots and hung them around their necks, along with gunbelts and other personal belongings.

Del's bedroll was so meager, he shoved his rifle into its center and lashed it across his shoulders, along with his six-shooter in its holster.

The night had remained humidly hot and the weird heat had increased, if anything, with the coming of daylight. The thunderheads had sailed closer, black and ominous. He could see them being torn by savage winds.

"We're goin' to ketch glory-be right soon," Tucson Slim said. "These here storms at daybreak generally turn out to be hair lifters."

"We ought to be in the clear before it hits," Rezin said.

"We better be," Shanahan said. "Mind the time Dave an' me was caught by a flash in the gorge. You fellers yanked us out with ropes, but I'm still shakin'. We lost not only our horses, but a lot o' steers, includin' my peace of mind."

Del looked at Kay. "Now, how about heading home?" he asked.

She might have been considering such a course, but that sparked opposition in her. "If these men can do it,

147

so can I," she said. She sat down and began yanking off her own saddle boots, preparing to drape them around her neck.

Rezin shrugged and grinned. "Next to a dead mule, there's nothin' harder to move than a female who's got her conceit on the prod," he said.

He glared around. "All right. The easy ridin' is over with. Throw 'em back on the trail."

He led the way southward again. Wan sunlight filtered momentarily through the clouds, then was blotted out.

Del discovered that Kay had joined him on the drag. She gazed up at the gathering storm, but refused to permit any outward sign of apprehension.

"I've always been told that nobody could get through the Cannons by heading straight south," she shouted above the rumble of hoofs.

"Both of us," Del said. "We still seem to be learning."

"Hike!" Rezin and Shanahan began shouting. "Hike! Yippee! Run, you fuzztails! Move! Move!"

Quirts and rope ends cracked. Del, with Tucson and Overmile, hazed the drag into a gallop and held them tight against the main drive. Kay lined up with them, a neckerchief drawn over her mouth to filter out the dust.

She was yelling and swinging a quirt. "Ee—yah! Get along, you misbegotten devils. Drat your hides, run! Run!"

The run became a wild avalanche. Rezin kept screeching, "Faster! Faster! Don't let 'em slow down! Haze 'em!"

The horses ahead were vanishing as though a knife was chopping off the column. Rezin and Shanahan vanished also.

Then Del saw the river. The Cannon. It emerged from

a gorge upstream and ran swiftly through an open stretch between a break in the cliffs. Like most southwestern streams, it was normally shrunken to insignificance in summer but was subject to quick, brief floods from the violent thunderstorms that were common at this season, especially in the mountains.

The Cannon was high and muddy now. In the Combabi country to the west, where it originated, it ran through wide, sandy channels. Here in the Cannons, through which it had found its way eastward, it was bottled in narrow gorges that in places were mere slits. East of the Cannons it lost itself in sands and arid deserts.

Del had never known that the river could even be reached in the Cannons. And though the Long Riders had found a way, this did not seem to be a ford. It had the aspects of a deathtrap. On their side, their route ended in a five-foot cutbank over which the horses were being rushed into the water. The river was narrow, no more than a long lariat throw in width, but there was no chance of landing on the opposite shore. Sheer rocks rose there with the current foaming against them.

He gazed downstream. Kay screamed in fear. The river swept into another gorge a few hundreds yards below. Nevertheless, the horses were still being hazed over the cutbank.

The animals in the water were swimming, but were being carried by the current toward the gorge below. Others were plunging in and rising to the surface, legs thrashing, white-eyed with terror.

Rezin and Jim Shanahan, astride their horses, which were swimming strongly, were forcing the column toward midstream. The chain of animals lengthened on the surface.

Tucson arrived with the drag, and spurred his mount into the water. Tim Buttons, however, reined up on shore and eyed the river dubiously.

"You fools" Buttons yelled. "That storm broke west o' here. There'll be a rise comin' down any minute."

Len Willis rode up and laid a quirt across the withers of Buttons' horse. The animal lunged over the cutbank. Animal and rider arose, choking and splashing water.

Buttons glared back and shouted something at Willis, but his anger was wiped out by thunder. Then came the rain in a torrent. Quinn and Cullen Camden, like Buttons, had halted at the cutbank and were staring disbelievingly at the river.

"If you think I'm going into that river, you're loco!" Quinn shouted at Del.

"Nobody turns back," Len Willis said. "That's the rule."

He used the quirt and sent Quinn's horse leaping over the brink. He spurred toward Cullen, lifting the quirt again. Cullen made a scornful gesture, then drove a spur to his horse and plunged into the Cannon.

Del remembered that Kay had told him neither of the brothers could swim. Quinn, gray-faced, clung to the saddle. Cullen, calmer, hung to the tail of his mount, letting the horse have its way.

"Go back," Del said to Kay. "Go home! This is no place for a woman." He grinned. "Not even for a lady."

"Thank you," she said.

She spurred her horse to the bank and forced it to leap into the river. She came up, still astride, caught her hat that had been yanked back on her shoulders and jammed it back on her hair, but too late to hold all the damp strands that fell loose. She gave Del a mocking look.

Del and Thane Overmile crowded the last of the

horses into the stream. "For once, I agree with Quinn Camden," Del said. "This looks loco."

He sent his horse into the water in a lunging splash. Coming to the surface, he left the saddle and clung to it, holding himself high enough so that his tarp roll received no further soaking, but offering little burden to his horse.

Kay was drifting with her mount a few yards away.

Farther on, Quinn and Cullen seemed to be in no difficulty.

But Tucson Slim was in trouble. His horse capsized .It rolled over and over in the water, legs splashing wildly. Yells of alarm arose from the Long Riders.

"Tucson's hung up in the surcingle," Rezin bellowed.

Tucson, a spur caught, was being rolled with the frenzied horse. He needed instant help, but no other person was within rods of him.

Del's .45 was within reach, draped across his tarp roll on his shoulders. He dragged it free, lifted himself a little higher. Tucson and his horse came to the surface. Both horse and rider were weakening—near drowning.

Del cocked the .45 and fired, praying that its brief immersion had not killed the cartridges.. His target was the head of the horse, but Tucson's head was also almost in the line of fire as he fought to free his spur. An error of no more than an inch would have told the story.

The bullet killed the horse. It stopped kicking, and floated limply on the surface for seconds. That gave Tucson the chance he needed and he wrenched his spur from the surcingle. He drifted clear of the dying animal as it sank.

He swam to Del's horse. Del caught his arm, pulled him to his side and they floated along, supported by the swimming animal.

"Pretty shot," Tucson said, after he could speak. "I felt the snap of air as it went past my eyes."

That was all. They drifted together. The episode was never mentioned again by either of them. And never forgotten. Del knew that if his bullet had killed Tucson its weight would have been on him the rest of his life.

The storm reached a climax. Lightning painted the sky an electric blue color. Thunder was deafening. Del looked downstream. The gorge below was frighteningly close at hand. He could see spray from a rapids.

He realized men were shouting, making themselves heard during lulls between the roar of thunder. Del's horse lurched, rising out of the water. It had found bottom.

A rope splashed within reach, thrown by Jim Shanahan, who had reached shore. He and Tucson grasped it and made their way through shallowing water to dry land. Nearby, Rezin had Kay by the arm, and was helping her to safety.

Del saw that they had been carried into an eddy that circled below a chain of rocks that thrust an elbow into the main current. A sizable side draw opened into the gorge at this point. From its mouth a talus slope fanned down to the gravel shore on which they had landed.

"Hustle!" Rezin was shouting. "River's actin' mighty strange! Trouble comin'! A flash, likely!"

Del saw that the majority of the horses had been carried into the eddy and were wading ashore. Quinn and Cullen Camden came splashing to dry land.

Leonard Willis, mounted, was in the river swinging a rope, hazing laggard animals to safety. Del waded to help him, for there were a score or more of horses still milling in the eddy. One was caught by the current and

152

carried downstream toward the gorge. Then another was swept away. And another.

Tucson came to help them. But it was useless. "Can't do anything for 'em!" Tucson shouted. "Let's get out of here! I feel grief comin' out of that draw upstream."

Del sensed it too—a deeper sound from above. He and Tucson fought their way toward shore, with Willis spurring his horse to their side in case they needed help.

They reached shore as a flash flood roared from the gorge upstream. The rise from the storm up the river had been jammed like a cork in a bottle between the walls of the canyon. The flash came out of the mouth of the defile in a sloping wall of water that was the sickly gray hue of wet slate. It carried snags and driftwood on its face.

Del and Tucson ran desperately. Willis attempted to drive straggling horses higher on the gravel slope. Two animals stubbornly dodged past him and returned to the margin of the stream.

Looking back, Del saw them swept away by the flash as it rolled past. A yellow tide was driven up the slope to tug at his legs. Kay, wading into the margin of the flood, caught his arm and tried to help him. It was help he did not need. But he enjoyed it.

The fury of the flash had already passed. The river was a brown, ugly snake, raging at its confinement, but it was already receding.

"We sliced that one a little thin, too," Del said, grinning at Tucson.

Tucson grinned back at him. "We did just that." Tucson sat down as though his legs had given way.

Quinn Camden was being sick in the background. Cullen was on his feet, trying to catch up his horse, which had yanked free and was circling aimlessly around. Jim Shanahan looked at the river and crossed himself. Rezin was smiling, as though he had enjoyed that joust with death. Len Willis, always fastidious, began shaping his drenched hat and was gazing ruefully at his soaked garb. He seemed unmoved by his narrow squeak.

Tim Buttons got his breath. He glared at Rezin. "You damned near got me killed, Bartee!" he panted. "You likely shortened my life. I got a bad heart. You had no right to—"

Rezin walked to him, grasped him by the arms, lifted him clear of the ground and walked toward the river with him. There was a terrible anger in Rezin, a Jovian fury.

Del stared, unable to believe that Rezin, the calm, slow-spoken one, really meant to cast Buttons into the flood, where he would surely be carried into the gorge.

He moved. He overtook them and touched Rezin's arm. "No, Rezin!" he said.

There was unyielding hardness in Rezin's expression. "You can't kill a worm just because it's a worm," Del said.

Rezin paused. He stood for a moment, debating it. Even Buttons quit squirming and yelling, awaiting the verdict.

Finally, Rezin lowered his captive to the ground. He sent Buttons reeling with a backhanded swipe—as he would swat an insect. "Maybe," he said to Del, "judgment will be in your hands."

Del didn't understand. Rezin offered no explanation.

"The Lord in His wisdom has been merciful," Rezin said to the others. "Once more we've been spared. Give thanks to the One who saw fit to help us safely across the waters."

Del was amazed. Then he bowed his head. For the Long Riders were joining Rezin in silent prayer.

"Amen!" said Kay.

Rezin again became the pilot of desperate men. "There'll be water an' graze about a mile or so up this draw," he said. "We'll hold the stock there 'til sundown."

"So this was the way Two Star beef was run into Mexico by you rustlers!" Quinn Camden said, regaining his bluster.

Rezin eyed him stonily. "One o' the ways. Nobody knew there was any chance of drivin' stock through the Cannons for miles east an' west o' here. But Dave Kittridge found that ford when be was chousin' wild cattle years ago in the Cannons. There were other trails the Long Riders used, but this one was the best."

"How many of our horses did you lose just now?" Quinn demanded. "I saw half a dozen or more being carried downriver."

"Take tally, if you're interested," Rezin said.

"And how many Two Star cattle did you thieves drown in the river the same way?"

"We lost quite a few," Rezin said icily. "Two hundred or more in one bunch once. That was part of the Big Raid. The cattle was spooked by a cougar that showed up on shore, an' they milled back into the river. We lost every head. But in the next few days we got the rest of the herd across an' into Mexico. Eight hundred steers."

"You've got the crust to stand there and admit you were the ones who pulled the big steal on Two Star?"

"We figured it'd sort of make up for Dave Kittridge bein' shot in the back," Rezin said. "But it didn't. We not only lost two hundred head of cattle, but two good men went into the gorge with 'em."

155

"The whole bunch of you ought to be strung up," Quinn raged.

Nobody spoke. He peered at the faces around him. His head suddenly hunched down into his shoulders as though he was in the ring, facing an onslaught. Cullen, aghast, whispered a warning to him to quit talking.

It was Leonard Willis who broke the silence. He spoke in a precise, judicial manner. "It is the rule of this group of men that any who travel with us who should be accused of, or suspected of treachery, or of doing or saying anything that might endanger the lives of the other members, or their future, be given a chance to explain and defend himself. If it is the unanimous decision that the accused man is guilty, then punishment will be decided."

"You're not scaring me!" Quinn said. But his voice was uncertain.

Kay spoke. She was ashen. She addressed them all. "He didn't mean it. He talks too much."

Len Willis ignored her. "This punishment can be either banishment from the Combabi or death." He added, "You're not accused, Camden—yet."

Del had opened his tarp roll and emptied his pockets in order to dry dampened personal belongings. The fingerless chamois glove lay among his effects, along with his shaving kit and spare garments but it was a shapeless item, partly covered and probably only Kay and Rezin were aware of what it really was.

Del felt ice inside. The glove had been little damaged by its immersion. If he were to pick it up and force it on Quinn's hand, it might be a sentence of death,

For these men who were gazing at Quinn, were warning him he was suspected of a crime they would not forgive— Dave Kittridge's death. These were not

156

the fellow citizens that the people of Combabi knew. These were not the mild lawyer, the choir-singing blacksmith, the owner of the gambling house, their law officer.

These were the Long Riders—reckless, chance-taking men who had lived outside the law in the past, and who had now reverted to their old ways. The code under which they had operated was again being invoked by them.

Del knew Kay was watching him. He saw the deep apprehension in her. She was waiting his decision. And Rezin was evidently leaving it entirely up to him.

He did not speak or move to pick up the glove.

Len Willis had quit talking and had turned away from Quinn. The moment of tension eased. The black cloud that had settled over the group passed by.

CHAPTER 13

THEY CAUGHT UP FRESH HORSES, ROUNDED UP THE scattered animals and moved them up the talus slope and along the bed of the creek in the draw whose sands were already swallowing the runoff from the storm.

The thunder had died, the rain had ended, and the clouds rolled eastward. The early sun came out. The draw broadened into a flat where there was forage. Cottonwood and willows straggled along the course of the stream. Rock pools held fresh rain water. Mesquite grew in the swales. Lonely ridges looked down on them, dotted with juniper, sage, and rabbit brush.

The willows became festooned with boots and belongings, drying in the sun. They built fires and ate what food they could salvage from the war sacks that had come through.

"As soon as the river drops back to anywhere near normal, Thane will build a raft of driftwood an' float our hulls an' hot rolls down," Rezin explained. "He's done it before. We'll take turns standin' watch at the eddy, so as to be ready to sling him a rope when he shows up."

Using the point of a twig, he drew a map in the sand. "Come sundown, we'll shove out. This draw cuts south for five miles or so. Then you cross a divide, an' drop down to open country. You've got a dozen miles of sagebrush to the border. That's where it gets mighty touchy. In the old days even the Rangers didn't bother much with that stretch, figurin' nobody could run stock through the Cannons. But every inch is bein' patrolled now by the Army. We don't know when, or how often they ride the line. That's a chance we've got to take."

Kay was busying herself, rearranging her soaked saddle jacket and hat on a boulder so that they would dry. Her jeans and shirt, still damp, clung to her figure. This was a comfort rather than a hardship in the growing heat of the morning.

Despite this, Del saw that she was shaking as though chilled. She was avoiding looking in his direction.

He went to her side. "You're shivering. How are you feeling? What's wrong?"

"Nothing," she said huskily. "I'm just being glad. Happy."

"How's that again?"

She choked up. "Thanks for again being merciful. To Quinn. About the glove. It might have sent him to—to his death. He might not have been the man who tried to kill you that night. I'm still almost positive that he never left the ranch after dark."

158

She could no longer hold back the tears. They stained her cheeks. "There's been enough mistakes. Too many people have died for—for nothing."

"Nothing? If you mean what Walsh Camden did to my father, do you call that nothing?"

"Of course not. But it was all so unnecessary. So pitifully unnecessary."

"It's a little late for excuses. And there's no excuse for greed. Walsh Camden is a greedy—"

"It was worse than greed. It was jealousy."

Del went silent. He knew he had opened doors beyond which stood grinning skeletons. He did not want to ask the next question. "Jealousy?" he echoed reluctantly.

"A woman's jealousy. And his own. Aunt Harriet hated your mother for marrying Dave Kittridge and bearing him a son. She hated you for being that son. And for being a better son than her own. She destroyed your parents, destroyed Uncle Walsh—and herself."

Del was appalled. "What are you saying?"

"She made Uncle Walsh what he is—a bitter, vindictive, friendless man. She made an outlaw of your father."

"Why? Why?"

"Because she was in love with your father."

"You can't be serious."

"I wish I was not. She never forgave him for rejecting her and marrying your mother, who had been her best friend."

"How do you know this? How long have you known?"

"Only since the other night before you came back to Two Star with word you'd got in touch with the Long Riders."

159

"Is that why you told me I was to blame for the feud?"

"Yes. Innocently to blame. As innocently as your father. As innocently as Uncle Walsh."

"Walsh Camden innocent? Now that's not to be—"

"He was driven to it by a woman who was almost out of her mind with jealousy and injured pride, Quinn gave me a hint of the truth that afternoon after you had left. I forced the whole story out of Aunt Harriet. I had half-suspected it for some time, but had refused to allow myself to believe it. It seemed too terrible, too monstrous."

Even though the other Long Riders had been out of earshot, Del saw that they were moving still farther away and were taking pains not to look in their direction. They could not help being aware that he and Kay were caught in a moment of great emotion and were taking elaborate steps to avoid being inquisitive.

Not so, Quinn Camden. He was staring, a derisive twist to his lips. Cullen, too, was gazing, a brooding speculation in his eyes.

"Quinn knows the truth too," Kay said. "And Cullen, knowing his mother, probably has guessed it."

"And exactly what *is* the truth?"

Kay had left grief behind her, and spoke tiredly. "My aunt was not in love with my uncle when she married him. She did that in a frenzy of anger after your father had married your mother. She was beside herself with jealousy. But she never gave up hope that she would prevail and that your father would come to her. It was her pride. Her damnable, selfish, implacable pride."

She paused a moment, then continued. "For a long time she pretended to accept the situation. She and your mother had been chums before they married, and Aunt

160

Harriet let this continue. The real reason was that this gave her the chance to visit at Rafter K often and therefore to at least see your father or be near him. The fact that he treated her with courtesy but always held her at a distance, maddened her."

"She actually told you all this?" Del asked.

"Not in so many words. I was able to wring from her only some of the facts. But it is easy to fill in the whole, terrible, tragic picture."

Del was gray-faced. "Go on."

"Aunt Harriet began to live in a world of her own within herself. Outwardly she was The Lady of Two Star, proud of her husband, her sons, and her position. Inwardly she seethed with rancor and humiliation. She began writing love letters to your father."

"Love letters! I can't believe—"

"Letters that your father never knew about, never even imagined. Letters that she never mailed. That she destroyed after they were written. Only she knew about them. They were a solace to her, a sort of safety valve. She was not normal, of course. She told me she even prayed that your mother would die."

"She got that wish," Del said harshly.

"In Aunt Harriet's case, time didn't seem to heal the wounds. Her determination only grew greater. She was living in a hell of her own making, pretending to be the loyal, faithful wife of Walsh Camden, and yearning continually for a man who treated her only casually as a friend and neighbor. At last, desperation drove her into the final mistake. She contrived to see your father alone, and tried to throw herself into his arms."

"Harriet Camden did that? The Lady?"

"She was rejected. Your father was a blunt man. He was shocked, horrified. He scorned her. Too bluntly, no doubt. For that changed her. Her obsession turned to hatred. I'm sure it had been hatred all along and that she had only deluded herself into believing it was love. She set out to avenge her humiliated pride. She saw to it that my uncle found one of the love letters she wrote."

"No human being would do that!" Del said hoarsely.

"You've heard of the fury of a woman scorned. This was the result. The letter was a lie from start to finish, of course. It made Uncle Walsh believe that she and your father had been carrying on this affair all those years. I believe you were about twelve by that time."

"The she-devil!"

"It was a matter of mistaken pride and jealousy. And not only on her part. Aunt Harriet isn't the only one who is self-centered, vain, and conceited. That was where Uncle Walsh was hit. What maddened him was that Aunt Harriet had married him only to spite your parents. The humiliation of learning that she had preferred another man all that time drove him wild. Aunt Harriet fed the fires by taunting him. It was she who incited him into smashing Rafter K. She even goaded him into showing your mother that letter."

Terrible fury blazed in Del. "Walsh Camden did that? I'll kill him! That was what sent my mother to her grave!"

"No. Aunt Harriet told me that your mother never believed it. Your mother knew Aunt Harriet's nature and she knew her husband. Aunt Harriet doesn't have your mother's death to answer for on that score at least. On another score, yes. It was seeing her husband hunted as an outlaw and knowing that it was all caused by a jealous woman that was too much for Lottie Kittridge."

She stopped talking. Del was swept by ravaging emotions. He pounded a fist savagely in a palm in an agony of futility as he looked back over the terrible years—the lost years. Years of seeing strong men at each other's throats, fighting to the death over only the distorted fancies of a vengeful woman.

"My God!" he said horsely. "My God!"

Nothing could change it. Nothing could open the graves on Castle Creek.

"But Harriet is paying," Kay sobbed. "She's been destroyed by her own whirlwind. She has come back to something like sanity—too late. She is horrified by what she started, but her awful pride will not let her admit to Uncle Walsh that she lied. In her own way, she's tried to atone. She's the one who has kept the graves of your parents green. She tends the plot secretly with her own hands. She's the one who burned the word 'murdered' on your father's grave marker. I believe it was to accuse herself."

"You say it was Quinn who gave you the hint of his mother's deviltry."

"Out of malice. He was furious because she insisted that he help save his father. After you had left Two Star that day, he came back and upbraided her. He let slip some of the things that confirmed what I had suspected."

She added, "He's inherited all of her bad points, none of her better ones. He's—he's—ugh!"

Del sat for a time, black blood raging through him. He arose suddenly and walked toward Quinn. In that instant he wanted to flail and slash. At destiny. At the mocking irony of it all. He wanted to erase that sardonic grin from Quinn's lips—from the face of derisive fate.

Quinn, startled, suddenly straightened, his hands instinctively shifting into an attitude of defense.

Rezin took a step, as though to interfere, then halted.

163

He glanced at his companions and made a gesture of acceptance.

Del said, "This is the time, Quinn. This is the place."

It came and went with cyclonic violence. He feinted Quinn into launching a punch that missed. He smashed aside Quinn's attempt at defense and landed two smashes to the jaw. All of his strength, all his anger against destiny's harsh ways were back of the blows.

Quinn reeled back against the stiff foliage of a juniper, then sagged forward on hands and knees. From that position he sprawled flat on his face.

Del turned and walked away. The chamois glove still lay shapeless and limp among his belongings. The black gust of fury had burned itself out.

But the futility of it all still was with him. Nothing had changed.

CHAPTER 14

DEL AND TUCSON SLIM RODE THROUGH SCATTERED creosote brush to the crest of a rise and dismounted. The hour was close to midnight, and the moon painted the land with bold brush strokes of silvery white and stark black shadows. Far ahead, massive shapes were inked on the horizon in hues of somber blue-black. Those mountains were in Mexico.

To the north rose the low ridges of the Cannons from which they had emerged after dark with the horses, and had felt their way into the open flats across which marched the white monuments that marked the international line.

More than half a mile behind them, the horses and the other members of their party waited while he and

164

Tucson probed ahead. They left their mounts round-tied, and moved on foot out of reach of any small sounds the two animals might make, so that they could listen.

The land lay so silent in the moonlight that their own pulses gave the impression that the vastness was alive and breathing. Waiting. Waiting for them, to engulf them.

"I'd say the only thing a man has to worry about on that stretch ahead is dog holes, rattlers, an' how to avoid fryin' to death when the sun comes up," Tucson murmured.

"On second thought," he added in a whisper, "I got creepen' feelin' there's somethin' out there."

"You're right," Del said. "An Army patrol."

"Where?"

"There, to the right. Now they're in the shadow of that ridge with the hump in the middle. They're swinging this way. Sit tight. Maybe they've spotted us. Maybe not. Don't run until we're sure it's necessary."

They waited. Presently, a file of riders appeared, looming on the crest of a swell, startlingly near. There were eight of them in loose formation. They passed on by, a pistol shot away, saddles creaking, bit chains jingling.

The faint tang of tobacco smoke lingered in the night as the cavalrymen continued their patrol westward. Del and Tucson began breathing regularly again.

"That," Tucson sighed, "made me start countin' my sins an' wishin' I'd never committed 'em. One sneeze by our horses an' there'd have been shootin'. All one-sided. If you ask me, I don't aim to throw any lead at the cavalry. I used to wear that uniform."

They returned to their horses and rode back to join the others.

165

"What's your guess, Del?" Rezin asked after listening to their report. "An' yours, Tucson? You two ought to know more about Army doin's than the rest of us."

"They're sure to swing back this way," Del said. "No knowing when. Maybe soon, maybe not for hours. It depends on how far west they ride before meeting the patrol from the other direction."

He added, "It's a chance we've got to take. Let's roll."

They crowded the horses into a run and headed them southward across the flats, Del kept his fingers crossed.

Their luck held. A white monument drew abreast, then fell astern as they kept the horses loping southward toward the blue-black mountains.

Eventually, they let the animals settle to a tired walk. They kept peering back, but it was not for another two hours, with daybreak lighting the rims of the rugged mountains ahead, that they began to really relax.

Rezin spoke to Del. "It's your sticky piece of cake from now on, *amigo*. We got you into Mexico. You know the way to Arroyo Grande better'n we do, I reckon. You're the ramrod of this drive."

Del looked across the backs of the band of horses at Kay who was riding on the opposite flank. She was wan with exhaustion, but was riding high in the stirrups, refusing to admit her weariness or to ask favors. She had held down her share of the task. No bunch-quitting horse had managed to break past her during the trying hours of the race from the Cannons across the line.

Cullen Camden also had held up his end, but Quinn had let three animals outwit him and escape into the night.

The sun came up. Del kept signaling a refusal whenever Rezin waved in his direction, requesting that they throw the horses off for a rest.

It was past noon, and Del had piloted the drive along the base of the mountain range which was now gray and forbidding instead of blue-black, when he gave the signal to halt at a small creek that flowed from the range.

"Tally out before we let 'em graze," he said. "Rezin. you and Leonard Willis keep count."

Jim Shanahan uttered a groan. "Man, you make a tough ramrod. What difference, how many we got? We're in Mexico with more'n I thought we'd ever make it with."

The tired horses were pushed between Rezin and Len Willis who sat in their saddles, keeping tally by the time-honored method of transferring pebbles from hand to hand.

"I make it two hundred and ninety-two," Willis announced.

Rezin nodded. "For once, the other fellow knew how to count as smart as me. I make it exactly the same."

"Eight short," Del said. "Not so good."

"What do you mean, not so good?" Quinn Camden demanded. "Torreón will be mighty happy to get his hands on that many."

Quinn's face was still puffed from the punishment Del had inflicted. He had never mentioned the speed with which he had been leveled and was beginning to regain some of his bluster.

"Torreón asked for three hundred head," Del said. "He'll be looking for an excuse, no matter how thin, to accuse you of failing to keep the agreement."

"To accuse me? *Me*?"

"I believe the man we came to Mexico to help is your father, isn't he? Remember?"

167

"And do you really think we can help him, now that we *are* here?"

"Maybe," Del said. "Maybe not. We can try."

"Just how do you aim to go about it?"

"There's only one way. Get in touch with Torreón and make sure first of all that your father is still alive."

He added, "I took it for granted you Camdens would want to do that."

"All we'd do would be to get caught in the same fix," Quinn said. "Torreón knows he's got us by the short hair. He'll never pay for these horses, nor turn the old man free. This is blackmail. He'll only ask for more horses, or whatever he thinks he can squeeze out of us."

"If you go into Arroyo Grande," Del said, "don't be easy to squeeze. That's the only way you can deal with Torreón."

"Talk's cheap," Quinn said. "I haven't said I'd go there yet."

"I'll go," Cullen exclaimed.

Del eyed him. Cullen had not taken a drink in days. His eyes had cleared and his mouth had lost its moist weakness. Like all the others, he was unshaven, his mouth taut with weariness. But he sat straighter in the saddle.

"I'll go," he repeated. "Where and when do we reach this place, this Arroyo Grande?"

It was not the vacation from the bottle that had changed Cullen Camden. Somewhere along the hard trail they had been following, he had found an answer to something. It was evident that he was suddenly standing on his own feet.

"It's fifty miles or less from where we now are," Del said. "We can be there before sundown tomorrow, with luck."

168

"There's no need for you to go any farther, Kittridge," Cullen said stiffly. "I've been told what will happen to you if Torreón gets his hands on you again. These other men can help us get the horses within reach of Arroyo Grande tomorrow. We Camdens can handle it from there on."

"I've got a personal matter to look into," Del said.

Cullen eyed his brother thoughtfully, as though never having really seen him before. "Go on back home, Quinn," he said. "Back to Two-Star. Keep playing at being a fighter. At being a man. This is no place for you. You might get hurt."

Del spoke. "Nobody goes back—unless we all go back together."

They trailed the horses southward at midafternoon. Kay rode at Del's side for a time. "This personal matter that you mentioned," she said. "Is it Amata Villareal?"

"Yes. I've still got to know for sure whether Torreón has really found her, or was faking."

"And how will you make sure?"

"I told you that I know where she is—or should be. There's the hut of a goatherder not more than half a dozen miles east of here. The goatherder is really her father, Luis Morales, who was once a wealthy man and a candidate for governor down here. He's the kind of a man Mexico needs—honest, dedicated to law and order and to the people. Fake *insurrectos* like Torreón and Antonio Carrosco try to get rid of men like Luis Morales, first of all. Up to now, he's managed to stay clear of their firing squads."

"Luis Morales was a guest of my uncle at Two Star some years back," she said. "I was about sixteen, but I remember him. He was so kind, so likable."

169

"He's tried to prod the *políticos* in Mexico City into taking real action toward stamping out these northern *bandidos,*" Del said. "But they're indifferent to what's going on up here. Luis Morales tried to organize resistance to Torreón, but had to run for his life instead. He disguised himself as a herder. Amata and her child should be with him at his hut. At least that was where Carlos told her to hide at the time the two of us were trapped and caught by Torreón."

"You're going there?"

"Yes. Tonight. I've been to the hut in the past when Carlos Villareal and myself were working with Morales at organizing his fight against Torreón."

She was thoughtful for a time. "What if you find that she's really in no danger and that Torreón was lying, just to bring you back into Mexico?"

"Is that a question?"

"Of course it is. Then there will be no reason for you to go any farther toward Arroyo Grande, as Cullen told you."

Del rolled and lighted a cigarette. "Let's just say that if this had come up a day or two ago, I might have turned back, everything being all right with Amata. But, since our talk, I've been looking at your uncle from a new viewpoint. Maybe Walsh Camden needs pity more than hatred. There's been enough hatred in the past, enough misunderstanding. He's had no easy time of it, either. He's suffered too."

He added, "Maybe more than any of us. Maybe more than he deserved. I'm going through with it now. I've had more experience in dealing with Torreón than any of you. I know the man and his nature. I'm going to Arroyo Grande."

She remained close at his side as their mounts moved

along at the walking pace of the drive. "I'm glad," she finally said, her voice husky. "And I'm afraid."

A seething urge for speed beset him. He began to fight the land—this wild, eternal, immovable land that was Mexico. The land that laid an eerie spell on a man. North of the line there seemed to be vitality, newness, the hopes and ambitions of a world that was still young and offering opportunity.

Here was a timeless country that gazed impersonally down on them. A land that was old and wrinkled and eroded by the winds, the rains, the suns of the centuries. A land of weird beauty, with mountains that rose, worn and somber like the rains of temples, with streams buried in mighty canyons, with skies bluer than any painter had ever achieved, laced with clouds of Olympian splendor.

Del had fought this land before, fought its silence, its cruelty, its unceasing weight. He fought these things now. Its miles were longer than other miles, its sun more torrid, its dust harder to bear.

He pushed the pace until Quinn uttered an angry protest. "Man, you'll kill us and the horses!"

He did not relent. He was one now with the land—with this Mexico. "Die then," he said harshly. "Ride, or die!"

He knew Kay was looking at him with somber dread. She uttered no protest, but pushed her horse along, stride by stride with his own.

Sundown came and dusk softened the face of the land. They reached water and Del gave the order to throw the horses off for the night.

He ate a meal that Kay cooked, her hands moving swiftly, for she now shared the burning impatience that roweled him. He saddled a fresh horse as the evening

171

star began to pale among the increasing glitter in the sky.

He had told Rezin and the others of his mission. They stayed apart, sensing that Kay wanted to be with him alone. She tested the cinch and the latigo with her own fingers as though this small, useless task would give her some measure of assurance during the hours of waiting.

She said nothing as he mounted. He let his fingers touch the warmth of her hair. Then he rode away, the .45 in his holster, the rifle in the boot.

CHAPTER 15

DEL SANK SUDDENLY TO THE GROUND AMID THE scattered brush through which he had been creeping, and lay flat. He judged that midnight was still an hour away. He had tied up his horse at a distance to the west and had made the final mile or more on foot. He was armed only with the .45 for the sake of easier traveling in the thickets.

He lay motionless. He believed he had caught the faint pungency of tobacco smoke. Now it was gone. It had been so elusive it might only have been imagination.

He waited. Ahead, the brush gave way to a clearing and he could make out the low shape of a goatherder's jacal, or hut, where the *cabrero* should be sleeping.

The tang of smoke came again, unmistakably. It brought memories. Memories of bivouacs in forgotten campaigns, of campfires, of roundup wagons, of bunkhouse talk and poker games. It was soldier tobacco that was burning. And cowboy smoke. The smoke of peons and vaqueros, of all the brown-faced, sun-swart men of the open spaces. Of patriots and of *bandidos*.

He crept forward a few feet at a time, fingering out his path ahead so as to avoid sound among the dry branches and leaves. This made tedious progress. Maddening and exhausting.

The moon, growing yellow with its decay, peered through the foliage with many slanting eyes. It was both a help and a peril. It lighted his path. It could betray him.

He had an advantage. The object of his stalk was not vigilant. He finally saw the bobbing movement of the peak of a straw *sombrero*—the hallmark of Juan Torreón's *soldados*.

Presently, he discovered a second hat and made out the glow of the tips of two cigarettes. He could now hear the faint murmur of soft talk. It was the desultory exchange of men bored with monotonous sentry duty.

The two presently flipped away the stubs of their smokes, shouldered their rifles and parted. One passed within a few rods of where Del lay, and vanished to the right, following the brush along the margin of the field that had been cleared for vegetables and a corn patch.

Del forced himself to wait a few minutes longer. The second sentry evidently had moved away in the opposite direction. The question Del had to answer was whether there were only two men on duty.

He decided that this was the case and that the two were walking a beat that circled the clearing and had common meeting places at opposite poles of their tours, However, he could not be sure he was right. There might be other sentries to deal with. And there certainly must be other *soldados* near—a squad detailed to watch the jacal.

He accepted the gamble. He crawled into the open

field. No sign of discovery came. Wriggling ahead, he reached a shallow ditch, dry now, that concealed him until he was within a stone's throw of the mud-walled hut. There he was forced to emerge again into the open.

The hut was dark and silent, its small window blanked out by a wooden shutter. Yet he was sure there was life within.

He crawled to the leather-hinged door and scratched on it with his fingernails. "Amata!" he whispered. "Señor Morales! It's Del Kittridge."

He heard bare feet on the clay floor. The door opened, and the shadow of a young woman in night dress loomed there. Her hand grasped his arm and drew him into the hut.

"*Madre de Dios*!" Amata Villareal breathed. "It is not possible! I have been afraid that you'd come. I have prayed that this would not be so. I have prayed on my knees, many times. Señor Del, my brave one, if there had been any way to warn you, I would have done so. It is a trap. We are being watched. Torreón's *soldados*. We had heard that he had released you. But his men are—"

"I know," Del said. "I crawled past them. Get dressed. And Carlota and your father? Are they here?"

"We are here, señor," a man whispered in the darkness.

"The *niñita* is here also." Both Luis Morales and his daughter spoke cultured English.

"You've got to pull out," Del said. "Now. As quick as possible. There are only two men on guard."

"They have been watching us for many days," Luis Morales said. "There are a dozen or more of them camped nearby. They pretend they do not know I am anything but a poor *cabrero*. They say they are an

174

outpost to, guard against raids by *bandidos*. They are *bandidos* themselves. They are here to see that we do not leave this place."

"Why hasn't Torreón grabbed you?" Del asked.

"There can be only one reason. They hope to seize others of my friends who might come here. Such as you."

"We might be able to slip away, if we move fast and quiet," Del said.

"But where can we go? We will only be overtaken."

"I've got horses for you, not far away. There's only one place for you. Across the line. You'll be safe in the States."

"You will go with us?" Amata exclaimed.

"No. I've got to go to Arroyo Grande."

"Arroyo Grande? But Torreón is there. With his *soldados*! He will kill you this time, like he killed my Carlos."

"I'll explain later," Del said. "There's no time now. Take only what you can carry. Don't light a candle. Make no sound."

"What a regret it is that this has to happen before the *federalistas* come," Luis Morales said sadly.

"*Federalistas?*"

"Of course. Have you not heard? They have finally ended their petty jealousies in the capital and awakened to their responsibility. The government is sending an army into the field to destroy these *bandidos*."

"Are you sure?"

"I am sure. The *federalistas* are commanded by General Manuel Escobar. An old friend. My troubles will be over when he arrives."

"I know Escobar," Del said. "A good soldier. But when is he starting this campaign? Where—"

"He arrived with three hundred men, horses, and supplies at Moctezuma by train some time ago and left there to march toward Arroyo Grande."

"Some time ago? How long?"

"I am not sure. The word was brought by peons, loyal to me, but uneducated. Ten days, perhaps. General Escobar spread the word that he was moving to capture the *insurrecto* Carrosco. In reality it is Torreón he hopes to strike first of all."

"Maybe these horses won't do Torreón any good, after all," Dell said. "Even if he gets them."

"Horses?"

"I'll tell you that story later also, Señor Morales. We should be starting now."

He kept watch through slits in the window shutter. The clearing lay silent and peaceful in the moonlight. Carlota, who had been awakened, sobbed softly until her mother cautioned her. She became silent. Carlota was only six, but danger and intrigue had become so much a part of her life that she obeyed her mother unquestioningly.

"I am ready, señor," Luis Morales said dryly. "I have my ragged hat, my empty purse, my peon's clothes and my machete. Fortunately for our purpose, I am no longer so endowed with possessions that they might be a burden to us in trying to make our way past Torreón's sentries."

"Carlota and myself are also ready," Amata said. A comely woman in her early thirties, she was brave, loyal, and dedicated to the cause for which her husband had died.

Del opened the door cautiously so that the dry leather hinges made little sound. The moonlight touched the cross that hung around Amata's neck. She wore the cotton waist and striped petticoat of the common people. Carlota had on the loose, coarse breeches and shirt of a boy and was barefoot. Her grandfather was similarly garbed, but had on rope-soled sandals. Hardship had aged him, Del saw.

Del led the way, keeping Carlota at his side. They crept across open ground to the ditch and followed it as far as possible. Del motioned the others to halt. They waited for a long time.

Finally, came the sign he had been awaiting. He saw the flare of a match in the brush at a distance. That marked the meeting place of the sentries. Tobacco smoke drifted to them. In due course, he saw the glint of a cigarette being flipped away and trod upon. He heard the two sentries parting. The faint sounds of their departures died away.

"All right," he whispered. He crawled from the ditch and they followed him across the open ground, enduring bruised elbows and chafed knees as they inched along on their stomachs. The brush arose ahead, offering shadows and shelter.

Del reached this haven first, with Carlota at his heels.

He got to his feet, thankful that they might now be safe.

He found himself facing in the moonlight a man wearing the uniform of a *capitan* in Torreón's *insurrecto* army. Marco Gonzales!

Recognition was mutual. Surprise momentarily paralyzed them both.

Then they were at each other's throats. There was no time to go for their guns. Gonzales was carrying a belted cavalry pistol in a holster, but the flap was snapped tight down. Del had swung his own belt and holster around on his back so that it would not impede

177

him in crawling. It was out of quick reach.

He moved faster than Gonzales. His hands clamped on the man's windpipe, dwindling the shout of alarm that was rushing up into an agonized grunt.

He drove a knee to Gonzales' stomach. Gonzales tore free of his grip, reeled back and managed to free the flap of the holster and draw his pistol. He would have killed Del then.

A machete flashed. There was the crunching. sound of steel biting deep into flesh and bone. Gonzales swayed. Del saw the terrible spurt of blood in the moonlight.

He picked up Carlota and shielded her from the sight of a man, already lifeless on his feet, falling, his body thrashing about in the reaction of violent death.

Luis Morales stood wiping the blade of his machete on a handful of leaves. "That one," he murmured, "betrayed my daughter's husband to his death at Torreón's hands. He betrayed you also, Señor Del. I apologize for seizing the right to exterminate such vermin. It should have been by your hand. But it was the hand of neither of us. It was the hand of justice."

Evidently, Gonzales was in command of the detail that was watching the jacal, and had come out from wherever his men were camped to see if the sentries were alert.

Knowing Gonzales, Del surmised that it had been he who had ferreted out the hiding place of Luis Morales and Amata and had put in Torreón's head the idea of using this as a club to bring back Del into Mexico as well as hoping that his connection with the Long Riders would ensure the delivery of the horses the *bandidos* needed.

Gonzales evidently had returned directly to duty after

178

escaping from the Combabi jail. The chances were that he had anticipated that Del would try to get in touch with Amata at her hiding place.

Del carried the child, and Amata assisted her father as they fled through the brush. No sign of alarm came. The *soldados* had not realized that their *capitan's* absence was being unduly prolonged.

They reached Del's horse. Luis Morales and Carlota rode while he and Amata walked.

It was daybreak when they sighted the horse herd. Breakfast fires had been lighted. Rezin and Kay mounted and came racing to meet them. Kay swung down, and took charge of the child who had fallen asleep in her grandfather's arms.

They then joined the others in the camp. "What's this all about?" Quinn Camden demanded. "What are we going to do with these people?"

"You might call them trumps for Torreón's ace," Del said. "But he's got another high card, of course. We're giving these people horses and sending them across the border where they can take sanctuary as political refugees."

He turned to Leonard Willis. "This looks like a job for a lawyer. I'd consider it a big favor if you'd see that these people get to Fort Griffin. I imagine you know the commanding officer there."

"My daughter and the *niñita* will go north," Luis Morales said. "But I will stay and continue the fight for my country. I will find the *federalistas* and join them."

Del nodded. "Of course. Provided there are any *federalistas* to join. Which I doubt. There's always been salvation just over the next ridge for Mexico. But nobody ever reaches the top of that ridge."

"I'll see that the señora gets safe across the line,"

179

Quinn Camden spoke. "You don't have to be a lawyer for a thing like that. I know the major at—"

He quit talking, looking at the faces around him. "What we ought to do is all of us head back for the line," he burst out. "Don't look at me like that. You know damned well that we'll only turn over horses to Torreón for a dead man. It can't be any other way. He's dead by this time. I'd bet my right arm on it."

"Speakin' of right arms," Rezin said, "there's somethin' that might maybe fit the hand you have on it."

Del knew there was no stopping it now. Quinn's insistence that they abandon his father had been the last straw with the Long Riders. Quinn did not realize it, but he was on trial for his life under the code of these men.

Rezin walked to Del's bedroll, opened it, found the chamois glove and pressed it into shape. Quinn watched, gripped by a sudden uneasiness. "What are you up to, Bartee?" he demanded.

He guessed that Kay knew. He turned to her, a sudden terror rushing up in him. "What is it?" he demanded hollowly.

Rezin walked toward him, the glove in his hand. Quinn began retreating. "Keep that thing away from me!" he yelled.

Tucson Slim and Jim Shanahan, grasped his arms and held him. Rezin began jamming the glove on his hand.

It did not fit. It was far too small.

Del's first thought was that perhaps the chamois had shrunk after its immersion in the river. But he had worn the glove himself as it had dried, just to prevent such a happening. Quinn was a big-boned man. His hands were bigger than Del had realized. It was obvious that he could never possibly have worn that particular glove.

180

He had not been the bushwhacker who had tried to assassinate Del.

Quinn backed away from the men who had released him. "What're you trying to do, to me?" He almost whispered it.

Nobody answered. Del heard Kay draw a sighing breath. He could see that the Long Riders were surprised. They had already judged Quinn guilty and had condemned him. Now, the death sentence had been repealed.

All except Rezin. He seemed more disappointed than surprised. There was a moody grimness in him that was difficult to interpret.

"You're a lucky man, Quinn," Del said. "You'll never be closer to it in your life."

He began stripping the saddle from his horse. "We've wasted time again. I'll need a fresh mount. Will someone rope me out one while I clean up some of those flapjacks?"

He looked at Quinn. "You're still going with us. To bury your father, if nothing else. You'll be shot if you try to turn back."

Riding at point, Del once more piloted the drive south. Ahead of them, Luis Morales, furnished with a horse, was vanishing into the distance, riding fast in his attempt to find the phantom force of *federalistas*.

Len Willis was lost from their strength also, having reluctantly agreed to escort Amata and her child to Fort Griffin. They were already on their way northward.

Kay rode again at Del's side. He was thinking that it had been little more than a week since he had passed over this route, on his way northward to Combabi with the message of Walsh Camden's predicament.

A week! It seemed incredible that so great a change

181

had come in so short a space. He remembered the intensity with which he had returned to the Combabi, intending to restore Rafter K and to smash the pride of the Camdens.

A somber desolation held him. All that was drained out of him. All that he had accomplished was to learn how futile it all had been. If Walsh Camden could have just bent a trifle and have admitted that the fault was his as much as his wife's . . . if only . . .

He felt Kay's hand on his arm. "Stop thinking," she said. "Stop trying to undo things that can't be changed. The look on your face frightens me."

She added, wonderingly, "Or maybe they *can* be changed. Even Uncle Walsh might change. Even he might admit the truth. For, deep inside, he knows the truth."

Before noon, riders appeared in the distance, circled the drive, then rode away at a long lope.

"Torreón's scouts," Del said. "They're carrying the news of our coming to Arroyo Grande."

Later on, other steeple-hatted horsemen appeared, but remained far away, staying abreast of them as they traveled.

They trailed the horses across the flat face of a grassy plain during the heat of afternoon. It was an hour before sundown when the plain ended, broken by the wide, yellow bluffs of an ancient water course that had carved a wide channel across the country.

They threw the horses off to graze and sat on their mounts on the crest of a bluff whose face dropped more than a hundred feet to the bottom of the arroyo, where the small stream meandered through sand flats.

Del pointed to the walls of a village which stood on a flat along the arroyo itself, not far away.

"Arroyo Grande!" he said. "And Torreón's *soldados* are still there."

The tents and picket lines of a ragged military camp flanked the village. There was antlike activity in the street and the plaza, with every face gazing toward the bluff to the west where the gringo horsemen had appeared.

Del peered southward, hoping for some sign of the *federalistas*. The country beyond the arroyo broke into rough hills and rocky ridges. It lay vacant in the late sun. The only movement on the yellow threads of the few trails was made by the burro strings of woodchoppers, packing their fuel to Arroyo Grande.

He called a council-of-war. He talked while he shaved, using water heated in a battered tin basin over the supper fire. He donned a clean white shirt, combed his hair and ran his hands over his smooth chin.

"I know how a sheep feels after shearing," he said. "But it's best not to look like a sheep when you deal with Juan Torreón. He's impressed by appearance."

He buckled on his gun belt. Jim Shanahan handed him a second belt, along with a weighted holster. "Torreón will be even more impressed if you pack double," the gambling man said. "That's a spare I've been carrying in my hot roll."

Del said, "Yes, and thanks," and added the second weapon to his equipment.

"If I'm not back by sundown," he said, "stampede the horses over the bluff and head, hell-for-leather, back toward the border. Keep remounts, of course, and stick close together. You'll make it."

They stared, shocked.

"This thing will be settled quick, one way or another," he explained. "If I get Walsh Camden out of

183

Arroyo Grande alive, he'll be with me when I ride back out of town. I'll wave both arms three times if everything is all right. If not, start the stampede."

Quinn Camden came out of his stunned silence. "Did I hear you right? Are you telling us to kill these horses? Nearly three hundred head of stock? Thirty thousand dollars' worth of animals?"

"What would you propose?" Del asked.

"Anything but that. We'll trail them back north with us."

"With a bunch of tired horses? How far do you think you'd get before Torreón's men caught up with you and took them from you? And slaughtered all of you to boot."

He added, "This is the only way. Walsh Camden rides with me out of that place before sundown, alive and unharmed, or Torreón will have a bunch of dead horses on his hands."

He turned to Cullen. "Agreed?" he asked.

"Agreed," Cullen said without hesitation.

He turned to Kay. "Agreed," she said.

Quinn started to frame another violent objection, but the expressions on the faces of Del and the others silenced him. "A hell of a waste," he raged.

CHAPTER 16

DEL MOUNTED TO LEAVE. CULLEN CAMDEN SWUNG aboard a horse and joined him. Del eyed him questioningly and said, "Are you sure you want to do this?"

"The Camdens climb their own mountains, wade in their own mud, pay for their own mistakes," Cullen said. "And kill their own snakes."

Suddenly they gripped hands and sat grinning at each other, not able to express what was in their thoughts.

"You shouldn't go into that place," Cullen said. "You know that, of course."

"Nothing could keep me away now," Del said. "It's a pleasure to ride with you."

Cullen leaned from the saddle and kissed Kay. "Thank you, Cullen," she sobbed. "Now the Camdens can hold their heads up again."

Tucson Slim also mounted and rode to their side. "I got me a shave an' a clean shirt too," he said. "Why waste such finery?"

He was carrying a brace of holstered pistols also. Black-handled .44s that were tied down. Lean, expensive equipment built for speed and precision that he must have kept protected in his bedroll to replace the lone rough-and-ready .45 that he had packed on the trail. Deadly tools. The tools of an expert.

The three of them rode away, side by side, toward Arroyo Grande.

Torreón's scouts, who had continued to shadow them, moved in closer. They were wild-featured, brown men, with crossed bandoliers on their chests, their tall hats adorned with bangles and relics of looted villages and ranchos.

Some of them recognized Del and began taunting him in Spanish. They asked him what brought the little mouse back to face the lion. They told him that the guns of the firing squad were thirsty for his blood.

Del called some of them by name, recounting deeds of less than valor that they had performed in battles. "It is not the lion you follow," he told them, "but the buzzard that feeds on the flesh of the people and

185

despises you because you fawn on him when he throws you the picked bones."

They fell silent and let him and his companions ride unchallenged into the crooked streets of Arroyo Grande.

The principal street was a dusty cart road that meandered among adobe huts into the plaza where a stone fountain spilled water into a round basin. A church lifted a bell tower.

Where the plaza had been crowded earlier with villagers gazing at the American horsemen in the distance, it was now deserted. All that moved were skulking dogs and chickens pecking in the dust. Two shaggy burros stood asleep on their feet near the fountain.

But they knew that ears were listening to the hoofbeats of their horses as they passed by and they sensed the eyes that peered at them from windows and from doors ajar.

They dismounted before the more pretentious of the adobe buildings in the plaza. This, according to its faded painted sign, was the office of the *jefe*.

It had two stone steps rising to its deep-set door. They mounted the steps and entered the building through the open door.

Juan Torreón sat lolling in a chair at what had been the *jefe's* wide writing table. The *jefe* was dead long since, his blood soaked up by the dust around the fountain where the firing squad had acted.

The table was scarred by the rowels of spurs and stained by spilled tequila and vino. A saber lay before Torreón on the table, its blade ground to keen edge so that it glittered wickedly. A heavy, German-made military pistol also lay on the table, with Torreón's thick, brown hand, adorned by two diamond rings, resting beside it, the fingers drumming a little military tattoo on the wood.

In the background sat a half a dozen of Torreón's officers who were aping their leader's indolent pose.

"Ah, it is my frien', el Señor Del Kittridge," Torreón said. He was always anxious to demonstrate his knowledge of English. "You have come back to join the army of *libertad,* no?"

Torreón had given himself the title of general, but he was wearing the commonplace khaki shirt and trousers that he preferred in the field. He was a wide, heavy-featured man with skin the color of old bronze. His eyes might have been cast from the same metal.

"This gentleman on my right is Cullen Camden, son of Walsh Camden, the man you're holding prisoner," Del said. "On my left is Tucson Slim."

"But el Señor Camden is not a prisoner, no," Torreón said in pretended hurt. "He is here on a matter of business."

Del and his companions glanced at each other. Walsh Camden apparently was at least still alive.

"We have some two hundred and ninety horses on the bluff down the river," Del said. "The price is one hundred dollars a head in gold, American. And the release of Señor Camden's father."

Torreón leaned forward, his eyes glinting with dry humor. "For a dead man, amigo, you speak impudently. I will grieve when you depart from us. And that will be within minutes."

He spoke to one of his officers without turning his head. "Bring the firing squad, *capitan*. This man was sentenced to die, and—"

"These horses will be stampeded over the bluff if myself and my friends and the Señor Camden do not ride safely out of Arroyo Grande before sundown," Del said.

The officer who had headed for the door, suddenly halted and stood staring.

"It would be a terrible thing," Del said. "I do not believe any of those beautiful horses would survive such a disaster. And, as I rode in, I noted that your own *caballos* are in poor condition. Pitiful, I would say."

Torreón, like a badger retreating into its burrow at the approach of danger, had withdrawn into himself. His grim humor had vanished. "They would not do this thing?" he growled. "Your *compañeros*? They would not do, what you say? Kill all those horses?"

"Those men back there on the bluff once rode with my father," Del said. "They are Long Riders. Surely, you must know that men like that would not hesitate."

Torreón's fingers were still drumming on the table— furiously now, angrily. He sat glaring. Seconds passed. A full minute. Del knew that Torreón was ransacking his mind for some solution—some way of checkmating.

"I hope you've got the money ready," Del said. "If not, that would be unfortunate. For my friends on the bluff have strict orders. Sundown. No longer. Once they are sure my friend's father is with us when we ride out, and that we have been paid for the horses, they will join us and we will all head north, leaving the animals for you and your men."

He added, "We have kept our part of the agreement The horses are here. Please produce Walsh Camden. I hope, for the sake of everyone, that he is still alive and that you haven't dealt too harshly with him."

Torreón brought both of his hands, palms down on the table with a frenzied crash. His voice, hoarse with fury, barked an order. The *capitan* went scurrying away.

Del looked at Cullen and Tucson. He could feel cold moisture in the palms of his clenched hands. They were still alive, at least. The odds had been that Torreón would have ordered all of them shot. But reason had prevailed on the *insurrecto* leader. Del surmised that his situation was worse than anyone suspected and that he had realized that he must temporize.

Presently the rhythmic slap of heels sounded. Walsh Camden was marched into the room at the point of a saber. He was bearded, thin and hollow-eyed and in rags. He was barefoot. His eyes were half-closed, pained by the open glare of light after weeks in a dungeon.

Cullen was at his father's side in fast strides. "Dad!" he exclaimed. "It's me, Cullen."

Walsh Camden uttered a choked sound that was almost a sob. Suddenly he was in his son's arms, clinging to him.

He got command of himself and straightened. Some of his old, austere, unbending dignity came rushing back. His moment of weakness was past. He seemed ashamed of it.

His eyes, growing more accustomed to the light, fixed on Del. He stood even straighter. "What's he doing here?" he demanded of Cullen.

"If you get out of this alive," Cullen said, "you'll owe it mainly to him."

"No," Walsh Camden said. "Not to any of that damned flesh and blood. I'll stay here."

"We've brought the horses you came down here to sell," Cullen said. "Unless we all ride out of this town soon, the Long Riders will run them over a bluff to their deaths."

"The Long Riders?" Walsh Camden said harshly.

"Don't tell me Dave Kittridge has come back to life!"

Del spoke. All the bitterness, all the anger of the past was suddenly back in him. "The murdered never come back. The dead never live again. How much did you pay the man who, shot my father in the back?"

He added: "Or did you save the price of the blood money by murdering Dave Kittridge yourself?"

"I could have killed him," Walsh Camden said stonily. "I *would* have killed him with my own hands, but only face to face. But he avoided me."

"I see no difference," Del said. "Bounty money is a license for murder. You put a price on his head. Some body collected that price from you."

"That's a lie. I never offered bounty on the life of Dave Kittridge or any other human being. Do you think I would pay a man for what I wanted the satisfaction of doing myself?"

"How can you say that?" Del demanded. "Everybody knows you offered the money for Dave Kittridge, dead or alive. Ten thousand dollars, so they say."

"And I say it's a lie. A lie that grew of its own weight. Wishful thinking, perhaps, on the part of men who wanted to earn that kind of money. I never offered a price on Dave Kittridge, even though he deserved it. He was an outlaw, a thief, a destroyer of a man's faith in his own household, a betrayer of his own friend."

"You're wrong, Father," Cullen said. "Dave Kittridge was innocent of those things. Entirely innocent.

"You don't know the facts, son," Walsh Camden, said.

"But I do. Mother told Kay the truth. The truth you refused to believe. You know it was the truth, don't you? It was only your pride, your conceit that wouldn't let you admit it, wasn't it? You refused to face the fact that she didn't love you when she married you, but was still infatuated with Dave Kittridge. It was your vanity that drove you to put the blame on a man who never knew why you had turned against him."

There was a silence. "Mother loves you now," Cullen said. "She's tried to make up for it. She loves you, I tell you. She was the one who wouldn't abandon you down here, Quinn did. I might have. We're here because she loves you."

Torreón and his staff had sat listening, fascinated. Walsh Camden looked at his son. His shoulders had lost their rigid assurance suddenly.

Del saw it. They were all aware of it. Walsh Camden was admitting the truth. For the first time, he was looking at himself fairly and honestly, and he didn't like what he saw.

Del turned to Torreón. "The money," he said. "Twenty nine thousand dollars in gold. Two hundred and ninety horses at one hundred dollars a head. We lost a few during the drive."

He gazed through the open door. The sun was low in the sky. The bluff to the west commanded the landscape. He could see mounted figures there, watching the town. Even at that distance he identified them—Rezin, Shanahan, Kay.

"I'd say you've got no more than twenty minutes' time," he said to Torreón.

He had the victory won. Torreón again brought his palms smashing down on the table in a gesture of infuriated defeat.

Then the thing happened that Del had hoped would not take place. Earlier, he would have welcomed the arrival of the *federalistas*. But now he had the issue settled without resort to guns.

191

A rifleshot had sounded. A volley followed. Then came the steady roll of gunfire. And yelling. The rattle of galloping hoofs.

Pandemonium broke out in Arroyo Grande. Women were screaming and children wailing. Men were running in the plaza. A bugle frenziedly sounded a call to arms.

"*El federalistas!*" a man screeched in the plaza. "*El federalistas!*"

Juan Torreón's reaction was characteristic of the man. He snatched up the saber from the table, ignoring the pistol. In this moment he wanted to see blood spilled. Del's blood.

For he knew that the horses Del had brought would never be his and the odds were that he would soon be lying dead in the plaza or facing a firing squad at sunrise.

He had no time now for vengeance on Walsh Camden, nor, indeed, any real motive. It was Del who had thwarted him, forced him to back down in the presence of his subordinates.

He came over the table in a savage lunge, the gleaming edge of the saber flashing as he struck.

Del drew both pistols, crouching and firing the .45s upward as the saber sliced through the crown of his hat, its edge brushing his hair.

His bullets tore through Torreón's chest, inflicting death as the *bandido* towered on the table. Torreón's body came crashing forward, his blood gushing from the wounds, the saber suddenly listless in hands that were paralyzed by the onrush of death. His body crashed to the floor almost upon Del.

The room erupted into deafening gunfire. Torreón's officers were shooting. Tucson Slim was kneeling beside Del, using the table as a bulwark while He fired

192

the brace of black, matched .44s. Some part of Del's mind marked how precisely Tucson was picking his targets and wasting few shells.

Cullen was at Tucson's side. He had pushed his father down and was crouching over him to shield him as he used his one six-shooter.

Del got to his knees. Across the room, three of Torreón's men were still shooting. Two were down. Another fell beneath Tucson's black scythe as Del started firing.

A rifle exploded in the doorway. A *soldado* had appeared there and joined in the battle. Del heard the bullet strike flesh at his side. He fired both of his pistols and killed the *soldado*. At the same moment the guns of the last two officers were empty. One hurled himself flat on his face, covering his head with his hands and shouting surrender. The other merely stood, gray-faced, expecting to be shot down.

Both Del and Cullen stayed their fingers on the triggers and spared them. Del turned. Tucson had quit shooting. He was swaying forward. Blood stained his shirt.

"Tucson!" Del placed an arm around him, supporting him.

Tucson looked up, and in his eyes was pride. "A good way to go," he murmured. "Alongside men who rode the river with me. No regrets. No regrets."

Tucson Slim was gone. Gone to the long sleep. Gone from the feuds and dark currents of a life of gunfighting and its treacheries and gray future.

Outside, the roar of rifles shook the walls of the town. Del scarcely heard it as he crouched there, looking down into Tucson's face. It was now a calm face. The crow's feet had smoothed, the eyes that still looked up at him were at peace. Tucson had found youth again.

Horsemen were crowding the street. They wore neat, green jackets and were superbly mounted and armed. Rurales, Mexicos best fighting force.

Cullen moved to Del's side and knelt, gazing down at Tucson. "I'm so sorry, Tucson," he choked. "So damned, hellish sorry. It should have been me."

Cullen was unhurt, as was his father. Walsh Camden was gazing down at Tucson with brooding sadness.

The plaza, for a time, was a tangle of horses and men, of gunfire and screaming and sabers flashing.

The battle swept past. It was almost over. The shooting was tapering off. The Rurales had swept into town from the brush across the river and the surprise had been complete. Torreón's ragged army of looters had been scattered and decimated in the first few minutes. The survivors were surrendering, or were being hunted down in the houses and even in the church. Some were fleeing on foot, with mounted men overtaking them. A deadly game of hounds and hare.

Del lifted Tucson's body in, his arms and walked out of the building into the plaza. Luis Morales stood there awaiting them. He removed his hat and held it over his heart.

Two riders came galloping up. Rezin and Jim Shanahan. They had come down from the bluff to follow the *Rurales* into Arroyo Grande. They dismounted and stood with Luis Morales, looking at Tucson in bitter silence.

"It should have been one of us," Walsh Camden said.

He looked at Rezin. "I always knew you were one of them, Rezin. One of Dave's men. And you too, Jim. Neither of you ever had any liking for me. Nothing but scorn. But it wasn't me who killed Dave. Nor any money of mine. Dave's son just accused me, but it isn't true. I know who killed Dave. He came to me, asking for bounty that I had never offered. It was one of his own men. A Long Rider. I never—"

"We know," Rezin said heavily. "He just told us the truth."

Del stared, appalled. "A Long Rider?" he said hoarsely.

Then he added, reluctantly, "Buttons! It was Buttons, wasn't it?"

"I figured you'd say that," Rezin said wearily. "At first I was sure it had been either him or Quinn Camden. Tim is a miser, a penny-pincher, a complainer. Him an' me never saw eye to eye. I always felt, deep inside me, that maybe he was the one that shot Dave for the bounty. That's why I forced him to come along on this run. I figured to get the truth out o' him. But I was wrong."

"Maybe I don't even want to know," Del said.

"The glove didn't fit Tim," Rezin said. "It fitted another of us. One I never suspected. About the last one I would suspect."

Del looked at him, waiting.

"Thane," Rezin said.

"Thane? Thane Overmile?" Del felt sick inside. "What are you saying? Why, Thane's the one who warned me—"

Rezin nodded. "That's what started me thinkin—when I really started to think, which was only today. Thane deliberately let Marco Gonzales escape from his jail that night. Then he came to me an' told me he'd better ride out an' warn you. What he was doin' was to set up a blind trail an' divert suspicion from himself."

"Suspicion? But, like you said, nobody had the

least—"

"Thane didn't know that. Guilty consciences are always jumpy, always seeing ghosts. Thane knew your father was alive that morning when you found him. He never was sure but what Dave might have been able to give you a hint as to who had shot him. He convinced himself you had come back to Combabi to pin it on him. So he tried to make sure an' the other boys would never suspect him. Likely he really aimed to kill you that night, but he'd warned you too well an' couldn't locate you in the brush. I happened to remember that he punches the bag for exercise, the same as Quinn Camden. He's got a bag set up in the jail. We tried on him the glove you found in the brush. It was his glove."

Rezin quit talking for a space. "That's what greed for money will do to men," he said. "To some men, that is."

"I wonder why Thane didn't try again to get me," Del said.

"Likely intended to. I figure that's why he agreed to come along on the drive. But he likely realized that you wasn't suspicious of him, an' decided it wasn't necessary to rub you out."

They saw another question in Del's eyes. Shanahan answered it. "No. He's still alive. It's like you once said. You can't kill a worm because it's a worm. And maybe we've softened with the years. We turned him loose."

He added tersely, "On foot."

They brought Tucson Slim back to camp at dusk in an ox cart they had commandeered in Arroyo Grande.

Kay embraced her uncle and kissed Cullen. She came to Del's side, kissed him and clung tightly to him. She remained with him, gripping his hand, while she wept for Tucson.

They dug the grave by lantern light, each man taking

196

his turn at wielding the picks and shovels they had borrowed from the *Rurales*.

Even Quinn, subdued, helped in the task. They all stood with heads bowed while Walsh Camden recited a prayer. Rezin sang a hymn, and a file of *Rurales* fired a soldier's salute over the open grave. Then the shovels became busy again.

They left Tucson there at dawn and headed north. Cullen was the last to leave the fresh mound of earth. He sat there on his horse for a long time before turning away to overtake the others.

The band of horses remained in Mexico, held by the *Rurales* until the legal complications could be solved. Far away, and to the west, Del saw a man afoot—a tiny speck in the immensity of the lonely land.

It was Thane Overmile, a man who would live the rest of his days alone—if he lived. For he had ahead of him miles of waterless desert under a blazing sun. In any event, he would never return to the Combabi country.

Cullen joined his father and they rode side by side in silence.

Walsh Camden straightened in the saddle and drew a deep breath. He seemed suddenly more sure that he would be able to face what lay ahead of him at Two Star.

But Quinn still rode apart from them, alien from them, not understanding them—or caring.

Del felt Kay's hand touch his. She was at his side. Ahead of them they could see the sun lighting the rims of the Cannons beyond the border. Their country. Their range. Where no longer the hatreds and false jealousies existed.

We hope that you enjoyed reading this
Sagebrush Large Print Western.
If you would like to read more Sagebrush titles,
ask your librarian or contact the Publishers:

United States and Canada

Thomas T. Beeler, *Publisher*
Post Office Box 659
Hampton Falls, New Hampshire 03844-0659
(800) 251-8726

United Kingdom, Eire, and
the Republic of South Africa

Isis Publishing Ltd
7 Centremead
Osney Mead
Oxford OX2 0ES England
(01865) 250333

Australia and New Zealand

Australian Large Print Audio & Video P/L
17 Mohr Street
Tullamarine, Victoria, 3043, Australia
1 800 335 364